"So it's all dead and buried between us?"

Dare's expression changed to one of lazy detachment as he spoke.

"Of course," Teal said carefully. "Feelings change—they die. Nothing lasts forever."

"How very philosophical." Dare dipped his head in a mocking salute. "So much so, in fact, that it almost tempts me to challenge it sometime."

The picture he presented was all too assured, too masculinely knowing, and in that moment Teal really hated him. Hated his male arrogance, his self-possession, his compelling looks. Most of all, she hated the effect he was having on her.

"Yes—well, if you've quite finished pandering to your ego, do you think we might return our attention to something of more interest to both of us. Like the reason for my being here," she said sarcastically.

Kerry Allyne developed wanderlust after emigrating with her family from England to Australia. A long working holiday enabled her to travel the world before returning to Australia where she met her engineer husband-to-be. After marriage and the birth of two children, the family headed north to Summerland, a popular surfing resort, where they run a small cattle farm and an electrical contracting business. Kerry Allyne's travel experience adds much to the novels she spends her days writing—when, that is, she's not doing company accounts or herding cattle!

Books by Kerry Allyne

HARLEQUIN ROMANCE

2527—SPRING FEVER
2593—SOMEWHERE TO CALL HOME
2647—TIME TO FORGET
2725—MERRINGANNEE BLUFF
2737—RETURN TO WALLABY CREEK
2761—STRANGER IN TOWN
2809—THE TULLAGINDI RODEO
2869—CARPENTARIA MOON
2929—LOSING BATTLE
2947—BENEATH WIMMERA SKIES
2990—MAN OF THE HIGH PLAINS

HARLEQUIN PRESENTS

743—LEGALLY BOUND
783—TROPICAL EDEN

Don't miss any of our special offers. Write to us at the following address for information on our newest releases.

Harlequin Reader Service
901 Fuhrmann Blvd., P.O. Box 1397, Buffalo, NY 14240
Canadian address: P.O. Box 603,
Fort Erie, Ont. L2A 5X3

Dark
Memories

Kerry Allyne

Harlequin Books

TORONTO • NEW YORK • LONDON
AMSTERDAM • PARIS • SYDNEY • HAMBURG
STOCKHOLM • ATHENS • TOKYO • MILAN

Original hardcover edition published in 1989
by Mills & Boon Limited

ISBN 0-373-03037-1

Harlequin Romance first edition March 1990

Copyright © 1989 by Kerry Allyne.
All rights reserved. Except for use in any review, the reproduction or utilization
of this work in whole or in part in any form by any electronic, mechanical or
other means, now known or hereafter invented, including xerography,
photocopying and recording, or in any information storage or retrieval system,
is forbidden without the permission of the publisher, Harlequin Enterprises
Limited, 225 Duncan Mill Road, Don Mills, Ontario, Canada M3B 3K9.

All the characters in this book have no existence outside the imagination of
the author and have no relation whatsoever to anyone bearing the same name
or names. They are not even distantly inspired by any individual known or
unknown to the author, and all incidents are pure invention.

® are Trademarks registered in the United States Patent and Trademark Office
and in other countries.

Printed in U.S.A.

CHAPTER ONE

THE DERWENT RIVER was sparkling in the early morning sun as Teal Hayworth set out from her apartment in West Hobart, and she hummed in time with the tune on the radio as she drove down the hill to the business heart of the Tasmanian capital below.

It was the kind of day that gave one's spirits a lift, and even though it was also her first day back at work after the Christmas/New Year break, her steps were light and eager when, shortly, she left the car park and began making her way to the office. She thoroughly enjoyed her work as an analyst/programmer with a firm of computer systems consultants, and not even the thought of remaining inside on such a beautiful day could diminish her enthusiasm for getting back into harness again.

No, the only fly in the ointment with regard to work was Claudia, mused Teal wryly as she journeyed upwards in the elevator. One or two birthdays short of Teals's own twenty-four years, and somewhat less qualified, Claudia was the most ambitious person she had ever come across, and made no secret of her desire to take over Teal's position . . . and her boyfriend, Dennis Elford, who both headed and had founded the consultancy.

To date, Teal had experienced no difficulty in keeping the younger girl at bay, on both fronts, but at

5

the same time it was a niggling drawback that engendered within her some feelings of unwanted tension on occasion, although none of it was present today when she stepped from the elevator and uttered a friendly greeting to the firm's young receptionist on entering the plushly carpeted front office.

'Oh, and Dennis asked me to tell you he'd like to see you immediately you came in,' the fresh-faced teenager added after returning her greeting.

Teal nodded. 'Did he say what about?' It would save some time if she already had the relevant file with her when she arrived at his office.

'Not exactly.' The receptionist shook her head. 'I got the impression it could be another contract. One he seemed extremely pleased about,' she relayed with an expressive grin.

'So what's new?' responded Teal, smiling humorously. 'Dennis is always pleased with all new projects.'

And why shouldn't he be? she pondered, continuing on to her own office in order to dispose of her bag before seeing her boss. In the beginning he had built up the consultancy almost single-handedly through a persistent belief in his own ability, sheer hard work and long hours, until now he was able to employ staff to relieve him of some of the workload, and Integrated Computer Systems were beginning to obtain a respected name in the profession.

Teal had been employed by the firm for just a year, and although not yet a senior in her field—she would need to complete further courses before being eligible for that classification—she was pleased with her progress to date. As her parents hadn't been able to afford to support her while she attended university full-time, she had been forced to take a job during the day and attend college at night. Fortunately, though, all those hours of study had started to pay off over the last couple of years, and made it possible for her to take her place in the team at ICS confident that she had something worthwhile to contribute.

Now, having deposited her bag in a drawer of her desk, Teal headed quickly for her chief's office, and was immediately greeted by an eager smile and the request that she take a seat.

'I clinched a new deal yesterday,' Dennis announced without preamble as she sank into the padded leather chair facing him. 'We had had discussions over the phone before Christmas, but as the business isn't actually located in Hobart, it wasn't until the owner was in town over the holidays that we could sit down and discuss the matter in detail.' He paused. 'And I'd like you to head the project.'

'Gladly.' Teal's reply was promptly made. 'I completed the last contract I was working on just before the break, so there's nothing to stop me from starting on this one right away.' She tilted her head, her brows lifting slightly. 'But it's out of Hobart, you said?'

'Mmm, closer to Launceston—your old home ground—as it happens. Near a town called Glenholme. Do you know it?'

'Well, I know of it, although I've never actually been there. It's in the foothills of the Great Western

Tiers, as I recall.' Then, with her gaze turning askance, 'But who wants a computer system designed for them?'

'A trout farm. The Calanda Trout Farm, to be exact,' Dennis surprised her by saying, and smiled at her wide-eyed expression. 'That's a new one for you, isn't it?'

'You're not wrong,' she agreed drily. 'So what kind of programs are they interested in?'

Dennis flexed a lean shoulder beneath his immaculate sand-coloured suit-jacket. 'Well, apart from the monitoring of automated devices—water pumps, feeders and so forth—to begin with it will mainly be rather basic: variations of spreadsheets, cost control, that type of thing, plus advice regarding purchase of the most suitable system. At least, that is unless it's decided to expand the system to take in control of, as well as just monitoring of, those automatic functions.' He drew a quick breath and leant forward a little, as if to lend weight to his words. 'I know you're really over-qualified for such initially elementary programming, but I want to be certain this project is perfect from start to finish.'

He paused, and Teal could sense that for some reason this particular contract meant a great deal to him. He wasn't simply pleased at having obtained it, as their receptionist had claimed; he was extremely excited about it, she realised suddenly. His finely sculptured features were far more animated than usual, his blue eyes glinting with an anticipation she hadn't seen since he had been successful in obtaining a contract for ICS with a group of state-wide motels.

'I'm hoping it will lead to bigger and better things in the future,' he disclosed at last in eloquent tones.

'Such as?' Teal probed curiously. Just how could a project for a trout farm, of all things, engender such hopes?

'Entrée to Tremaynes!'

The importantly announced revelation had Teal's stomach lurching. Just the name of one of Tasmania's largest family business concerns was sufficient to bring back memories still, even after five long years. Dark memories for the most part, painful memories she had tried so hard to forget. But Dennis didn't know that, of course, and he was obviously expecting her to be as enthusiastic about the prospect as he was. Schooling her features into a suitably impressed mould, she forced herself to eye him directly.

'By what means?' she queried, if somewhat tautly. 'Presumably the trout farm isn't one of Tremayne Industries' subsidiaries if it's privately owned . . . as I gathered it was from what you said. So where's the connection?'

Dennis sat back in his chair, his whole attitude one of triumphant satisfaction. 'The connection, my sweet, is the owner himself.' He paused, evidently wanting to give the utmost significance to his following disclosure. 'Who just happens to be none other than the elder son and heir . . . Dare Tremayne!'

'Dare!' The name slipped involuntarily from Teal's lips in horrified accents, her careful control abruptly crumbling as she sprang to her feet without thinking,

to begin pacing agitatedly about the room. 'You mean
that's who you're expecting me to work with on this
project?' She shook her head in fierce rejection. 'I'm
sorry, Dennis, but I just can't do it! You don't know
what you're asking of me!' She turned to face him
urgently. 'Please . . . give the project to someone
else. Claudia, for instance. She would jump at it, I'm
sure.'

'More than likely,' he conceded, frowning, and
patently nonplussed by her unexpected and
uncharacteristic behaviour. He had always considered
Teal's level-headed approach to problems and her
businesslike manner two of her greatest assets.
'However, apart from her not being free to undertake
any extra work at the moment, I wanted someone I
could trust implicitly in charge of this project.
Someone with *your* reliability, *your* thoroughness . . .
and Claudia isn't yet in that class.'

At any other time Teal would have been gratified to
have heard him say so, but unfortunately not on this
particular occasion. 'Well, someone else, then,' she
proposed flusteredly. 'There are others here equally
reliable and thorough.'

'But all of whom are already fully engaged with
other work at present,' Dennis disposed of that
avenue of thought decisively. 'And to be honest, I
really can't understand why you're making such a fuss
about the matter. OK, in view of your reaction, I
assume you met, or knew, Dare Tremayne at some
time. Now I come to think about it, you did actually
work for Tremaynes some years ago, didn't you?
Although why you should allow that to have any

bearing on here and now escapes me. What's past is best forgotten.' He paused. 'As, I might add, would appear to be the principle Tremayne also follows, because when I mentioned your name in connection with the project he didn't say so much as a word.'

'You told him I would be his analyst/programmer?' Teal gasped.

He nodded. 'Mmm, and not by any sign did he indicate that he even *knew* your name, in fact.'

Meaning that, among all the other female scalps he had collected, she had indeed meant so little to him that not even her name registered with him any more? A needle of pain lanced through Teal at the thought—to her annoyance, and consternation. Good heavens, why should she care whether he remembered her or not? She had certainly done her best to put him out of her mind completely over the years, and quite successfully too, she had believed.

The most important thing was that she had the career she had always wanted, and her allegiance was to Dennis now . . . and he was relying on her. How could she even consider letting him down when she could see just how much it meant to him?

'In that case, I guess I can do no less,' she declared resolutely at length, and finally resumed her seat. There was a moment's hesitation, and then she offered on a deprecatory note, 'I'm sorry to have acted so irrationally. It was just so—so completely unexpected, that's all.'

Although Dennis seemed relieved by her changed attitude, his expression still didn't clear entirely as he continued to survey her carefully set features in a thoughtful fashion. 'You did know him—quite well, though, I gather?' he hazarded.

Teal swallowed and avoided his gaze. She supposed she had unthinkingly made that much obvious, and there was little to be gained by prevaricating. 'We were—involved in a relationship for about three to four months,' she owned throatily. Determinedly she brought her gaze back to his, her mouth shaping obliquely as she attempted to make light of the matter. 'When I first started work at Tremaynes as a dewy-eyed trainee programmer.'

'And he still means something to you?'

Teal's eyes softened. Was that what he was thinking? 'Heavens above, no!' she denied forcefully. 'Until you mentioned his name, I hadn't even thought of him for years!' At least, she had certainly tried not to, came the silent amendment that had her giving a dismissive shake of her head in response. 'No, Dare Treymayne means nothing to me any more. He's merely a reminder of an impulsive, youthful indiscretion I would rather hadn't happened,' she added firmly, as much for her own reassurance as for his.

Dennis nodded. 'Then you shouldn't have any trouble in being able to work with him?'

Teal released a heavy breath. Of course it would be difficult. Dare had aroused emotions within her such as no other man since ever had—including Dennis. She had been in love with the man! Passionately, hopelessly in love with him, so that after their break-up—admittedly instigated by herself—she had even left Tasmania altogether and gone to live with an aunt in Melbourne for a number of years, in order to ensure that there was no chance of their accidentally coming into contact again as she struggled desperately to forget him, to get him out of her system.

Nevertheless, that was all in the past and best left there, as Dennis had proposed, she now reminded herself decisively. When all was said and done, she wasn't the same impetuous, inexperienced teenager she had been then. She was a capable career woman in control of her own life and feelings—despite that momentary lapse caused by the shock of suddenly hearing Dare's name again—and one who had a reputation for being crisp and poised in her attitude, definitely not lacking in assurance or composure.

So what if it was a little difficult? She surely had enough control to rise above that, hadn't she? Not to mention sufficient pride and self-respect to refuse to allow Dare to believe their brief affair had meant any more to her than it evidently had to him! Moreover, by now, at thirty-one, he would doubtless be married, and therefore even less likely to want to recall the past than she was—an unexpectedly thought-provoking prospect that she discarded swiftly. Deliberately she returned her attention to the man on the opposite side of the desk.

'No, now that I've had a few minutes to become accustomed to the idea, and to put it into perspective, I don't envisage any trouble at all,' she declared determinedly. 'As far as I'm concerned he'll be just another customer with just more programs for me to write and implement.'

'That's all I wanted to hear.' The last of Dennis's

doubts finally disappeared as he smiled in obvious relief. 'So when could you be ready to start? Tomorrow?'

So soon! Regardless of her last statement, Teal would still have preferred just a little longer to prepare herself. 'I—well . . .'

'I thought you could collect whatever you need from here and then spend the rest of the day packing and driving up to Launceston,' Dennis interposed. 'You'll stay with your parents, I presume? Then you'd be able to drive out to the trout farm from there each morning. I understand it's only a thirty- to forty-minute drive from the city.'

'Yes, but . . .' A chance thought occurred and her glance turned whimsical. 'I understood we were supposed to be going out to dinner this evening.' At least, that had been the arrangement when she had last seen him a few days ago.

Dennis looked suitably abashed. 'So we were,' he recollected. 'But this is business, and possibly very important business to the firm, at that.' His glance turned cajoling.

Teal sighed ruefully, knowing that whatever was in the firm's best interests was always Dennis's prime consideration. A trait that was quite the reverse of Dare Treymayne's attitude towards his family's enterprises, the involuntary and somewhat acid comparison followed. As she recalled, Dare's preoccupation had just about wholly centred upon enjoying the good life!

Why, even now she found it difficult to credit that he was actually involved with this trout farm. It sounded like work, and that was something Dare had never had any penchant for! At the same time, however, the fact that trout were involved was the only thing that did sound appropriate, she allowed sardonically. Him and his damn trout fishing! She couldn't remember the number of times that pastime had generated arguments between Dare and his father on his parent discovering that his eldest son had, yet again, absented himself from the company's offices in order to indulge in that considerably more favoured pursuit.

Not that any of it mattered to her now in the slightest, except in so far as it related to her work, of course, she told herself with some asperity, vexed at the direction of her thoughts.

'All right, since it's so important to you, I'll let you off on this occasion,' she answered Dennis at last. Besides, she supposed the sooner she started this project, the sooner it would be finished. Then, with a mock-threatening gaze, 'But it had better not become a habit.'

'It won't, I promise,' he assured her, smiling, and starting to his feet. Moving around the desk, he reached Teal as she rose upright herself, and looped an arm about her shoulders. 'It's only a postponement, not a cancellation.' His features sobered slightly. 'I'll miss you while you're away, you know.'

'Although only until you become absorbed in your next program design,' Teal retorted on a deliberately light and teasing note as they made their way to the door. She liked Dennis and enjoyed his company, but she still wasn't sure she was ready to become deeply involved again with any man just yet.

'You do me an injustice, and underrate yourself,' Dennis chided, but in wryly resigned accents that showed he was well aware of her wish to keep their relationship casual and uncomplicated at this stage. 'None the less, if you do feel in need of my assistance, for *any* reason at all . . .' he was meaning to include any problems she might have concerning Dare, Teal was certain, 'you know you only have to ask, don't you?'

She nodded and smiled fondly at him, touched by his consideration.

'Then I guess there's nothing more to be said, except to wish you well and . . .' he bent his head to brush his lips briefly against hers, 'to remind you to hurry back,' he concluded softly.

'Oh, you can believe I'll be doing that!' Teal averred with feeling. 'Just as soon as it's humanly possible.'

She hadn't ever wanted to renew her acquaintance with Dare Tremayne, but, now that she had no choice, she didn't intend that it should continue for one minute longer than was absolutely necessary!

If it had been possible, Teal would have preferred to live at home with her parents all the time. She had a very good relationship with her parents and liked the company they provided, but unfortunately when she had returned from Melbourne some eighteen months previously she hadn't been able to find a suitable position in Launceston, and so had been forced to look for opportunities in Hobart instead, just as she had when first starting work.

The fact that the two cities were only three hours' drive apart did allow her to drive home for the weekend every so often, although on this particular morning, as she prepared to drive out to the trout farm for the first time, she could only wish that it was a different set of circumstances that was allowing her to spend more time with her family.

Never had she experienced such difficulty in deciding just what to wear, she realised vexedly as she finally donned a slim-fitting tailored dress of navy blue linen trimmed with white. Nor did she usually take quite so long with her make-up and hair, she recognised with growing irritation on surveying her appearance in the mirror of her dressing-table.

She was a tall girl of some five feet six inches, and the dark material of her dress seemed to emphasise the slenderness of her waist in comparison to the rounded swelling of her generous breasts, the slim skirt to accentuate the length of her shapely legs. Her honey-blonde hair was cut short and layered close to her head, a thick sweep that curved across one side of her smooth forehead, softening what otherwise could have been a severe style. Beneath widely-winging brows, deep blue eyes, now shaded with discontent and an undeniable trace of nervousness, stared back at her from between surprisingly dark, long and curling lashes to which high cheekbones gave a somewhat exotic slant. Her nose tended to be tip-tilted, her firm jawline depicting a certain stubbornness, while her mouth was wide and curving, with a shape that enticed. It dominated her face, thereby giving it an arresting quality rather than a conventional prettiness.

Would Dare think she had changed very much? Would he still find her—attractive? Teal abruptly discovered herself to be wondering, and promptly emitted an appalled gasp before berating herself roundly for even considering such thoughts. By all accounts she had made such an impression on him last time that he hadn't even remembered her name when Dennis had mentioned it, so what made her believe he would recognise her either? In fact, it would be a relief if he didn't! While as for him finding her attractive . . . Why should she care if he did or not? Was her ego really that much in need of flattering—it never had been before—or was it because subconsciously, and regardless of her assertions that Dare Tremayne meant nothing to her any more, she *wanted* that attraction to be there still?

'Oh, how ridiculous can you get?' Teal immediately snapped contemptuously, the force of her feelings making her voice her disdain aloud.

Of course she didn't want him to be attracted to her! It had simply been a stupidly idle and totally unwanted musing, that was all. Good lord, she needed a complication like that in her work with Dare like she needed a toothache! With a disgruntled scowl she turned quickly to snatch up her shoulder-bag and briefcase from the bed, and stormed towards the door.

'If you—umm—feel up to it, give our regards to Dare, won't you?' requested Mrs Hayworth tentatively of her daughter as she accompanied Teal out to the garage a few minutes later. Teal had explained to her parents on her arrival the night before exactly who she was required to work with on this particular project. 'I—I know how difficult it was for you when the two of you broke up, even though it was your decision, but . . .'

'But at the same time, he was always very pleasant to you and Dad,' Teal finished for her in wry tones, and her mother nodded.

'You're sure you don't mind, though?'

Teal shook her head. 'Whatever was between us happened a long time ago, Mum, and I'm over it now.' If she could just be rid of the memories too . . . Purposely abandoning that line of thought, she kissed her mother's cheek and opened the door of her red Astra. 'However, passing on your message could be a wasted exercise, in any case, since I understand he doesn't even remember my name,' she added, sliding behind the wheel and depositing her bag and briefcase on the passenger seat.

'Not remember your name?' Mrs Hayworth exclaimed, taken aback. 'But of course he does. I don't know why he wouldn't, when he remembered your father's name very well when they met a few months back.'

'Dad met him?' Teal gazed at her parent in astonishment. 'Where? You never said anything about it to me.' Her voice turned a trifle accusing.

Mrs Hayworth looked apologetic. 'We thought it best not to, knowing how you—how you . . .' She gave a meaningful shrug and continued, 'Anyway, it was only the once. While fishing up at Great Lake.' She paused, smiling expressively. 'You know what a keen trout fisherman your father's become since he retired.'

What male in Tasmania didn't at some time or another? thought Teal ruefully. The island was a legendary trout angler's paradise that drew fishermen from all over the world to try their hand at catching that aristocratic fish. With so many different and superb localities to choose from—the central highlands alone were known as the 'Land of Three Thousand Lakes'—the not uncommon possibility was of an angler having a whole lake shore or waterway to himself, thus ensuring the fish were not over-exploited, it was hardly surprising that it was a sport that enthralled so many in the State.

And provided it remained a sport, to be indulged in during weekends and holidays—not become a way of life almost, as it had with one particular person she could name!—Teal had no argument with the pastime.

However, it wasn't until a short time later, after she had joined the freeway heading south, that the full significance of her mother's disclosures registered with her, and in consequence raised a number of disturbing questions—the most disquieting revolving around whether her father had happened to mention that she worked for Integrated Computer Systems.

If he had, it could explain why Dare had given no reaction when Dennis had mentioned her, and even perhaps why he had approached ICS in the first place intead of Tremaynes' usual consultants. A circumstance she had been inclined to think somewhat strange. Simultaneously, though, in the unbelievable event that she did happen to be the reason Dare had gone to ICS, there immediately rose the even more worrying question . . . why?

For revenge in some fashion, because she had walked out on him? Teal shook her head dismissively. That was hardly likely after all this time, surely? Nor was any other motive she could think of either, she was forced to concede eventually, when nothing logical came to mind. No, it was all just a freakish coincidence, nothing more.

In any case, wouldn't she be better disposed to solve the problems she did have, rather than attempting to deal with those that probably didn't even exist? Because, in spite of all her reassurances to herself about being in control of her feelings, Teal was only too aware of the knot of tension beginning to form in her stomach, and of the increasing clamminess of her hands as they gripped the wheel tighter the closer she came to her destination.

She had left the freeway some time ago, the road she was now following gradually becoming narrower as it crossed the verdant, undulating farmland that gave on to the thickly wooded foothills of the Great Western Tiers. At the small township of Glenholme the road forked, a sign in the centre designating the Calanda Trout Farm some three miles distant to the right, and Teal headed the Astra slowly in that direction. Whether in an effort not to miss the farm, or in an attempt to simply delay her arrival, she wasn't prepared to decide.

As it happened, she doubted she could have missed it even if she had tried, because the signs outside were impossible to overlook. Turning in through the wide gateway, she made for the small, flower-surrounded stone cottage that appeared to serve as a kiosk-cum-entrance at the edge of the surprisingly large parking area. On alighting from her car, she made herself stand for a moment, breathing deeply to rid herself of the annoying feeling of edginess that was gripping her, and making a show of looking about her interestedly. Even so, barely anything registered other than the wide expanse of landscaped lawns that lay beyond the cottage, and which were intersected by gravelled paths, a number of long, sunken ponds, and a variety of trees and shrubs.

To her left, from the direction of the stone building, came the sound of a door closing, followed almost immediately by a male voice that was so incredibly familiar that it had Teal's breath catching in her throat. It was as if the last time she heard it had only been yesterday!

'Well, well . . . so you didn't back out of it, after all!'

CHAPTER TWO

DRAWING on her deepest reserves of control, Teal turned slowly, her gaze painstakingly steady as it came to rest on the jeans and maroon T-shirted muscular figure standing with easy negligence, hands thrust into back pockets, only a yard or so away. She had forgotten how tall he was, she acknowledged inconsequentially. Even though she was wearing high heels, he still towered over her. Everything else about him seemed much the same, however, she noted with a strangely sinking feeling. He was still as dangerously attractive as she remembered.

Beneath the dark brown hair, his well-tanned features were firm, clear-cut, compelling. His mouth was finely etched, with an openly sensuous curve, and Teal felt a tightness in her chest on recalling his heart-shaking smile. None the less, it was in his eyes that the greatest danger lay. A tawny shade of amber flecked with gold and bordered by dense, overlong lashes, they gleamed with a recklessness, a devil-may-care audacity, that she knew from past experience could prove all too devastatingly lethal.

'Were you hoping I would?' she replied at last, countering his faintly mocking look with one of pseudo-amused disdain.

Dare shrugged a powerfully built shoulder. 'Not hoping . . . merely expecting.' His mouth curved obliquely. 'I thought it more than likely you would prefer to . . . remain on the run.'

His implication was obvious, and Teal sucked in a sharp breath. 'Except that I never did consider it "running", Dare . . . even in the first place!' she retorted on an ungovernably flaring note.

'Well, what *would* you call it, then, when someone takes off without so much as a spoken word, let alone a bloody written one? And not only that, but promptly scuttles out of the damn State as well!' he derided.

'I called it sensibly cutting my losses! And apart from my departure having perhaps damaged your ego slightly, don't bother telling me you cared, because we both know a failure to find willing female company has never been one of your problems! Quite the opposite, in fact.' A trace of bitterness surfaced.

'Meaning?' Dare sent her a keen, watchful look.

Teal shook her head. She didn't want to rake over the past, and nor had she intended to, until he had made that remark about her running away and she had been unable to prevent herself retaliating. But now, she hoped, she had her emotions back under control once more.

'It's not important,' she claimed in an offhand tone as a result. 'It all happened a long time ago, and I'm really not interested in resurrecting it. All that concerns me is getting on with my work . . .'

'Well, nothing's changed in that regard, at least,' he reflected in sardonic tones.

Teal stiffened in response to the sensed criticism. 'And why should it have changed?' she demanded. 'It's the reason for me being here. Besides, I enjoy my work, and it's always been important to me.'

'To the exclusion of just about everything—and every*one*—else, you forgot to add!'

'I resent that.' Her temper rose waywardly once more.

'I'm sure you do,' he acceded smoothly. 'Too close to the truth, was it?' One well-shaped brow quirked infuriatingly upwards.

Teal's hands clenched at her sides, her nails digging into her palms. It was all she could do to stop herself responding physically to the goading look on his handsome face.

'No, it was not!' she denied fierily with her tongue instead. 'But even if it was, at least trying to *make* a career is a good deal better than carelessly neglecting one in order to go fishing all the damn time!'

Dare's eyes suddenly seemed amused. 'I'm not sure why it should apparently matter to you, if that was my choice.' He paused, his head tilting slightly to one side. 'I didn't ever neglect you, did I?' he quizzed in a softly meaningful voice that, to her despair, immediately evoked images she had been at such pains to forget.

Pictures of them together in happier days, of passion-filled nights when she had so welcomed his possession. Pictures so strong that, abruptly, it seemed as though her fingers could still feel the hardness of his muscled frame beneath their sensitive tips, as if her body still recalled the unquestioning rapture in feeling him deep inside her . . . A burning warmth raced through Teal, shocking her out of reverie. Was she utterly out of her mind?

'N-no, you didn't ever neglect me,' she just managed to stammer, albeit somewhat throatily, at last. Valiantly pulling herself together, she continued on a crisper note, 'Anyway, that isn't the point.'

'I thought it was,' he remarked drily.

Teal pressed her lips together. But she hadn't put her career first, as he contended . . . had she? Oh, of course she hadn't, she assured herself stoutly. He was simply attempting to use it as an excuse to justify his other contemptible behaviour.

She had always known how effortlessly Dare attracted the opposite sex. Hadn't she fallen prey to the same undeniable appeal, too? Nevertheless, the totally unexpected discovery, by way of an item in the social pages of a newspaper, that she wasn't the only female he was romantically involved with at the time, had been completely shattering. The more so in view of the fact that he had been the one to pursue *her* when they had first met, and because he had never once even given a hint that he had found their relationship anything but as satisfying as she had.

Not that she had ever really anticipated anything lasting coming from it, despite having fallen so deeply in love with him. She *had* put so much time and effort into her work and studies—was still doing so!—that she had wanted to continue with her career. Moreover, nor had Dare made any mention of any long-term commitment either. Considering the opportunities the Tremayne name alone afforded him to pick and choose, had she really expected him to? But, notwithstanding all that, she had expected him, evidently naïvely, to at least be honest with her. The devastating discovery that he hadn't had been the cause of her resigning from her position with Tremaynes the very next day and leaving the State altogether just twenty-four hours later.

'Well, whichever way you choose to view it, this is getting us nowhere,' she now condemned in her most businesslike manner. 'It might be more productive if you began telling me something about this place.' She swept her eyes cursorily over the grounds once more and, in retaliation for his having resurrected such painful memories, gibed dulcetly, 'Daddy bought you some fish of your own to play with, in the hope of keeping your interest on work that way, has he?'

Momentarily, Dare simply steadily returned her goading gaze, his tawny eyes gleaming with a promise of retribution that made her breathing quicken, and then he gave a mirthful laugh.

'Don't be malicious, my pet,' he chided humorously. 'It doesn't suit you.'

His teeth were white and even in his suntanned face, and, feeling her every sense treacherously and chaotically responding to the vital magnetism he exuded so carelessly—just as they had done so often before!—Teal fought desperately against its effects, infuriated with her own foolishness in thinking she might have been able to discomfit him in some way.

Had Dare ever taken anything seriously—including herself? And, because he didn't, she should have known better than to even attempt to get under his skin. His free and easy nature made him impervious to any such taunts. Lord, even his own father's criticisms regarding his casual attitude towards their family enterprises had always been like water off a duck's back!

'And you wouldn't have a clue any more what suits me or not, Dare,' she snapped squashingly at length, channelling her ire in his direction.

Taking a step forward, he caught her off guard by suddenly catching her chin and lifting it, his glance lazing over her sensuously for what seemed an eternity. 'It could prove interesting to find out, perhaps,' he murmured implicitly.

Disconcerted more than she would have thought possible, Teal snatched free of his warmly disturbing grasp and strove frantically for an air of indifference. 'I doubt it,' she rejected as coolly as she was able. 'Nor, might I add, does it happen to arouse *my* interest in the slightest.' To deny him the opportunity to comment further, if indeed that had been his intention, she turned back swiftly to her car in order to retrieve her bag and briefcase. 'Now, what does claim my attention . . .' She allowed her words to trail off significantly.

'I know. Your work,' drawled Dare in the driest of accents.

Teal's head lifted. 'Well, we do have other clients' needs to attend to, so I don't exactly have unlimited time at my disposal.'

'That's not the impression I received from Elford,' he promptly disabused her. With considerable satisfaction, she suspected vexedly. 'He was most emphatic that you would remain here until I was quite certain I had—no further use for you.'

Despite the expressive pause that rankled even

further, Teal steeled herself against replying in the manner she was tempted to. His comment had also been an opportune reminder of just what Dare's business meant to Dennis, and the importance he placed on it.

'Yes—well, still only within reason, of course,' she had to make do with in consequence.

'Naturally,' he had no compunction in conceding, aggravatingly. 'Did you think I meant otherwise?'

Teal forbore to answer. Damn and blast him! she railed silently in lieu. He evidently didn't intend to make the time they were forced to spend together any easier, and it incensed her to realise that, notwithstanding all her resolutions to the contrary, he was able to unsettle her so effortlessly. For heaven's sake, she was twenty-four years old, not an inexperienced teenager any longer!

'It will undoubtedly take an unreasonable length of time, nevertheless, if the start continues to be delayed,' she put forward on a determined note. 'So shall we begin with the . . . kiosk, is it?' She raised an enquiring brow even as she set off purposefully for the stone building a short distance away.

'Plus souvenir shop and entrance,' elucidated Dare, keeping pace with her, and confirming her own earlier assumptions.

'The farm is open to visitors, then?' she commented, having already deduced as much from the fact that there was a kiosk. It also explained the unexpectedly large parking area.

'Very much so,' he endorsed, holding open one of the two glass doors that gave on to the slate-tiled entrance area. 'They're quite a profitable sideline to the whole operation.'

Giving an acknowledging nod, Teal preceded him through the doorway, scanning the interior quickly.

For the most part it consisted of one long room, the largest section of which was set with tables and chairs for the serving of light refreshments. Multi-paned windows provided a pleasing aspect of the farm, complete with a large and decorative fern-encircled and trout-filled pool alongside the building. The remainder was taken up with a glass-fronted counter displaying the souvenirs Dare had mentioned; the shelves on the wall behind it divided by two doors that provided access to the kitchen and a storeroom, and containing more souvenirs as well as the usual assortment of packaged confectionery and snack foods. To the right another door stood open, leading into the grounds.

Apparently having heard their entry, a young girl of little more than seventeen, but with an extremely well-endowed figure, now appeared in the doorway of the storeroom, her red-gold hair making a vivid splash against the darker fittings behind her.

'Ah, Amy. Come and meet Teal,' Dare invited. And after a full introduction had been made he went on to explain for the older girl's benefit, 'Amy runs the kiosk just about single-handed.'

'And I'm Dare's favourite girl, aren't I?' the redhead inserted brightly, looking to her employer for corroboration before turning her dark brown gaze somewhat archly in Teal's direction.

Precocious and possessive as well, thought Teal

wryly. The remark also made it obvious Dare's bachelor status hadn't altered during the intervening years. But to make her own position quite clear as well, she remarked deliberately with a friendly smile, 'That's nice. I'm *my* boss's favourite girl too.'

'Oh, are you?' Amy seemed relieved at the knowledge, her expression becoming noticeably more genial.

On the other hand, Teal was only too aware that Dare was regarding her intently, although she adamantly refused to return his gaze. Resolutely she kept her eyes glued on Amy instead, and forced her mind back to matters of business.

'I expect you're looking forward to the time when the computer's actually installed and operational,' she surmised amiably.

To her surprise, the teenager gave an unimpressed grimace. 'Not really.'

'Amy would prefer matters to remain as they are,' it was left to Dare to disclose drily. 'She reckons she doesn't need any machine to tell her what's going on.'

'Oh, but it will make it so much easier for you,' Teal tried to convince her. 'Keeping records of everything you sell, stock on hand, profit margins, details of suppliers, numbers of visitors; it can include whatever information you require and in any combination you choose, plus enabling you to assess that information at a moment's notice and allow you to see it at a glance.' Halting, she smiled reassuringly. 'Believe me, working with a computer can not only save you a tremendous amount of time, but it can be very enjoyable as well.'

'Enjoyable?' echoed Amy in a tone that patently indicated how difficult she found that to believe.

'Mmm. Apart from anything else, it's very pleasing indeed when you want a copy of some information, and it prints, word-perfect, in a matter of minutes what it would otherwise take you hours or even days to reproduce . . . *and* all while you're off doing something else, I might add.'

Amy appeared to give some thought to the prospect. 'But I can't even type,' she advised at length in doleful tones.

'Don't worry, neither can a lot of people when they first start using a computer keyboard,' Teal returned with a laugh, hoping to put the other girl's mind at rest on that score at least. 'But you learn after a while, once you become more familiar with it. In any case, if you think it might still be a problem, I can always make it simpler for you when designing the system by arranging it so that you can use symbols or abbreviations in the kiosk's particular program.'

'You can really do that?' Amy's expression lightened considerably.

Teal smiled and nodded. 'That's what I'm here for. To ensure you get the program you want, and can work with comfortably.'

'Well, I think you've just gone a long way to breaking down Amy's opposition to computers,' remarked Dare a few minutes later when he and Teal left the kiosk to continue their tour of the complex. 'Thanks. I was beginning to think she'd never come round to accepting the idea.'

Nettled by the warm feeling that stupidly enveloped

her at one mere word of appreciation, Teal gave a deprecating shrug. 'You don't have to thank me,' she rebuffed stiffly. 'As I said to Amy, that's just part of my job.'

'To keep clients happy?'

Teal's breathing deepened. Had there been a subtle edge to his query, or was it simply her imagination getting the better of her because of her own undeniably tense state? To cover herself, she pushed out a simulated laugh.

'With our program designs? Of course!' She made herself continue. 'There's little to be gained in designing programs that immediately create user resistance because they're too difficult, or too complicated.' She paused, and something she couldn't control had her casting him a highly expressive glance and mocking, 'Especially when a customer's— favourite girl is involved.' Her lips curved sardonically. 'You always did like them young, didn't you?'

Dare came to an abrupt halt, a partly amused, partly ironic laugh issuing from his tanned throat. 'Come off it!' he exhorted with a trace of scorn. 'That's merely an expression, nothing more. Hell, I've known Amy since she was a kid of twelve, and think of her in terms of a sister more than anything. Whereas in your case, my pet . . .' he cupped her neck with a warm hand, his thumb caressing the soft skin possessively, and there was a suddenly sensuous look in the ebony-lashed eyes holding hers that released swirling emotions within her she was helpless to overcome '. . . my feelings were of an entirely different nature, I can assure you.

And, I might add, there was considerably less difference in *our* ages.'

Teal moistened her upper lip with the tip of her tongue, her gaze seemingly finding it impossible to break free of his. 'I—well, from her manner Amy certainly gave the impression that she . . .'

'Wishes to read more into our association than mere friendship?' He shrugged negligently. 'No doubt lack of encouragement will have that dying a natural death in time. And that's with, or without, your effort to distance yourself from the whole affair.' With slow deliberation he brushed a finger along her jaw, setting her pulse pounding. 'So you're Elford's favourite girl, are you?' he drawled with an idleness Teal found strangely suspect.

'More or less,' she owned faintly, and was promptly unable to comprehend why she hadn't been more positive. 'We—we've dated a number of times, but neither of us wants to rush into anything we might regret later.' It was only a half-truth, of course, but she was sure Dennis would understand.

'Meaning you're not sleeping together yet?' A lazy mockery tugged at the corners of Dare's mouth.

His words were fortunate in at least one aspect, Teal discovered. Luckily, they snapped her out of the disconcerting trance she seemed to have lapsed into, and her temper flared, making her blue eyes flash as she stepped swiftly back from him.

'Not that it's any concern of yours, but as a matter of fact, no!' Spearing him with a withering look, she went on in caustic tones, 'I've already made that mistake once in my life, and I'm not about to repeat it!'

'Once bitten, twice shy, huh?'

'Precisely!'

'And does Elford know I'm the reason for your—er—reluctance?'

Teal eyed him with the coolest dignity she could muster. 'He's aware we had an involvement many years ago, yes,' she answered, albeit indirectly, but with some pleasure, none the less. If he thought she had tried to keep their relationship a secret from Dennis, then he could think again.

'And he still had no objection to you coming here?' A dark brow quirked expressively.

Teal shrugged. 'Why should he have? He also knows that whatever was between us happened, and finished,' inserted purposely, 'a long time in the past. Dennis realises that I'm a totally different person now, and that I view this project simply as work for just another client.'

'I see.' Dare's expression altered to one of lazy detachment. 'So it's all dead and buried between us, is it?'

Despite the casualness of his tone, Teal felt a shiver of tension suddenly crawl along her spine. There was just something about him—in his stance, maybe, or the measuring, gold-flecked depths of his eyes—that made her wary.

'Of course,' she asserted carefully, and therefore not quite as forcefully as she would have preferred. 'Feelings change—they die, are outgrown—as others rise to take their place. Nothing lasts forever.'

'How very philosophical!' Dare dipped his head in a

mocking salute. 'So much so, in fact, that it almost tempts me to challenge it some time.'

Teal's stomach constricted and her breath staggered in her lungs, but with a supreme effort she faced him back with pseudo-calm. 'Except that attempting to rekindle a spark in a long-dead fire is always a futile task . . . not to mention an utter waste of time,' she returned in meaningful accents.

Dare merely smiled unconcernedly. 'Maybe . . . maybe not,' he drawled.

The picture he presented was all too assured, too masculinely knowing, and in that moment Teal really hated him. Hated his male arrogance, his self-possession, his compelling looks. But most of all she hated the effect he was having on her: the destruction of her composure and the turning upside-down of her emotions. It was unfair that whatever she said failed to dent him, while he . . . he appeared to have the power to wreak havoc with her every resolve—it was no good denying it—with just a look or a touch.

'Yes—well, if you've quite finished pandering to your ego for the day, do you think we might return our attention to something of a little more interest to both of us? Like the reason for my being here!' she said sarcastically, and, turning on her heel, set off along the path once more.

Behind her, Dare made an unrepentant sound of reproval. 'You're being malicious again, my pet,' he admonished in taunting accents.

Teal sucked in an irate breath and came to a rapid halt, swinging back to face him heatedly as he approached at a more leisurely pace than her own had been. 'Deservedly, I would have said!' she sniped. 'And I'll thank you to remember I'm not *"your"* anything, Dare!'

'Not even my systems consultant?' he bantered.

Teal grimaced vexedly. He had her there, damn him! 'All right. Yes, I'm that,' she allowed grudgingly. 'But nothing on a personal level, Dare. Nothing at all, do you understand?' Her voice rose frantically.

Not that her protest had much effect, however. Dare merely flexed a muscled shoulder and infuriatingly made a substitution as he acceded facetiously, 'OK, precious. If you think Elford would object . . .' He shrugged again.

'Dennis has nothing to do with it!' she rounded on him immediately. '*I'm* the one objecting!' Her jaw jutted a little. 'And you're just being deliberately annoying!'

'Successfully too, it would appear, if that's the case,' he wasn't averse to goading as he mockingly surveyed her smouldering expression. 'But don't let it make you lose heart. After all, there's always a light at the end of the tunnel, as they say. So if the going should happen to get too tough, you can always take the easy way out—*again*—can't you?' His voice held a wealth of derision. 'Since you're Elford's favourite girl, I'm sure he would prove only too understanding if you said you just couldn't hack it any more.'

Teal wasn't so certain Dennis's reaction would be anything of the kind. He would be far more likely to simply find the aggravating effect Dare was having on her inexplicable—as she did herself to some degree!—and once again suggest she just disregard everything other than her work. But Dare wasn't to know that, and besides, she had her own dignity and self-esteem to consider as well. His last insinuation had rankled.

'Oh, yes, you'd like me to admit defeat, wouldn't you? In retaliation for having walked out on you last time, I suppose!' she scorned. 'Well, nothing doing, Dare! There's not a thing you can say or do to make me lose heart any more, and I'll be seeing this project through to the bitter end, regardless.' She drew a deep breath. 'And while we're on the subject . . . quite frankly, I fail to see how you've the hypocritical gall to judge my actions when *you're* nothing more than a moral desert!'

'A moral desert?' There was sardonic laughter buried in his voice even as he gazed at her askance. 'All because I didn't view my work with the same degree of single-mindedness that you did yours?'

His obvious amusement had Teal's resentment escalating. 'Among other things!' she slated with an implicit glare.

Dare's eyes narrowed slightly. 'Such as?'

She shook her head in rejection, already ruing her gibing outburst. The last thing she wanted was to prolong the conversation. 'It doesn't matter any more. In fact, I would prefer to forget all about it,' she rejoined curtly. 'It's over with. Finished. My only regret is that I foolishly permitted you to nettle me sufficiently into saying anything at all in the first place.'

'That's as may be,' granted Dare ironically.

'However, I might remind you that it's usually customary to allow the condemned man to know exactly why he's been convicted.'

Teal pressed her lips together. 'And usually the condemned man is aware of that only too well . . . no matter how he might like to feign ignorance!' she retorted.

'And just what's that supposed to imply?' His tone turned unexpectedly sharp.

Unconsciously, Teal's head angled higher and she held his gaze unflinchingly. 'Whatever you like,' she declared with a studiously indifferent shrug. As if he didn't already know, anyway! He was simply averse to acknowledging that she had found out about his two-timing activities! 'Personally, I find digging up the past totally unprofitable . . . not to mention unutterably tedious.'

At her deliberately snubbing manner, Dare's expression hardened, his gaze skimming over her insolently. 'Mmm, since your own behaviour wasn't precisely above reproach, I guess it's not surprising you're reluctant to discuss it,' he mocked promptly—but not lazily this time. Rather it was an acid, cutting mockery that sliced like a knife. Unbearably tempted to retaliate with her most scathing words as a result, Teal only just managed to stop herself in time.

Instead, she staunchly coerced her lips into an aloof half-smile and said with admirable calm, 'Then in view of our apparent differences of opinion regarding the past, I suggest we restrict our comments to the present from now on . . . just as I originally intended.'

She glanced about her significantly and then lifted a questioning brow. 'So—once again—shall we continue with the work in hand?'

Dare bent his head briefly in response. 'It would appear the most appropriate course to follow . . . at least, for the moment,' he conceded, to her relief, even if that feeling was somewhat tempered with a certain wary apprehension brought about by his last words.

CHAPTER THREE

AS THE MORNING progressed, however, Teal discovered that it just wasn't always possible to avoid all reference to the past—for either of them.

Sometimes a remark would simply come spontaneously, sometimes with an ungovernable deliberation—those on her part always immediately censured—although fortunately none engendered any further recriminations of a purely personal nature.

Consequently, by the time she had deposited her bag and briefcase in the ground-floor office of the delightful Georgian-style sandstone house that had been the original homestead on the property, viewed the various large and unbelievably well-filled ponds that were set into the grass, and which separately contained both the breeding stock and maturing fish, as well as inspected the incubators and assorted fry and fingerling tanks in the hatchery—the nucleus of the whole operation—she was beginning to feel able to relax a little and to act more naturally. As evidenced by her comments on returning outdoors from the hatchery.

'Oh, that man and woman and their two children have fishing-rods and creels with them!' she exclaimed in surprise, seeing the group making their way between some of the shrubbery. 'They're not allowed to fish here, are they?' She had already noticed some tourists looking over the farm, but nothing like this foursome.

Dare's lips twitched. 'The sign at the gate does say Calanda Trout Farm *and* Fishing Complex,' he advised wryly.

'Oh!' Teal said again, feeling a little foolish. As she recalled, she had been too tense to pay the sign much attention at all on her arrival. She hurried on protectively, 'But why would they pay to come here to fish—and presumably pay for their catch too,' a nod confirmed her assumption, 'when just about every lake, river, and creek in the State is full of trout that can be caught for free?'

'Mainly because not everyone, particularly tourists in general, has unlimited time at their disposal to not only locate a likely fishing spot but spend hours waiting for the bite that might not come—and that's only if the season isn't closed at the time owing to spawning—but would still like to try some angling, all the same. So they come here instead, where, with almost two tons of fish to every pond, they know for certain they'll be successful and the fish they later eat is fresh.' He indicated a tree-shaded picnic area at the base of the hill that formed one boundary of the farm. 'There are also barbecues available if they feel like cooking their catch here for lunch, as well as a playground for the kids, and if they so wish they can also receive coaching on the finer arts of angling.'

'From you?' Teal glanced at him from the corners of her eyes.

Dare's head dipped briefly. 'As well as Laurie Debenham. He's Amy's father and together with his wife, Martha, they live in the new house past the picnic area. Laurie's been with me since the venture first started. You'll meet both him and Martha shortly when we visit the packing shed.' There was a slight pause, and a bantering smile slowly etched its way across his firm mouth, lazily teasing, and wholly captivating in its effect. 'So you see, all those hours spent fishing have been put to good use, after all.'

Momentarily, Teal looked away, disconcerted by the rush of confusing emotions that assailed her. Oh, lord, why after all this time did he still have the power to tighten her stomach into knots? she despaired. He made her feel vulnerable and out of control—feelings she hadn't experienced for years—and it mortified her that he could unnerve her so. Why couldn't she just ignore him, for heaven's sake? With a shiver, despite the heat of the summer sun, she faked a small smile as she compelled her gaze back to his.

'You do actually work here, then?' she hazarded on a defensively sardonic note.

Dare laughed, his teeth gleaming whitely. 'You'd better believe it!' he drawled. 'This is my baby. Conceived and developed by me . . . and put into practice with Laurie's assistance.' He arched a graphic brow. 'Or didn't Elford tell you I was the owner?'

'Well, yes, but knowing your past attitude towards work . . .' Her previously somewhat fixed smile uncontrollably assumed a dulcetly explicit cast.

Dare's expression suddenly sobered. 'Mmm, work involving industry, retailing, the media, mergers, take-overs . . . and interminable boardrooms,' he listed with unanticipated but obvious dissatisfaction. His mouth took on a crooked tilt as he fixed her with a glance that came close to derogatory in its irony. 'You never did realise that those circumstances didn't constitute everyone's idea of the pinnacle of success, did you? That others did actually measure success by other criteria than yours!'

Teal gasped, her cheeks burning as much as her indignation. 'Then if that was the case, why even start at Tremaynes?' she flared.

Dare expelled a heavy breath. 'Because I knew that was what my father had always wanted.'

'You never mentioned anything like that before.' She eyed him with a suspicious frown.

'Maybe because you never enquired,' he returned pointedly. A mocking curve caught at the corners of his mouth. 'You were always too busy telling me how fortunate I was, as I remember.'

'Well, so you were!' retorted Teal immediately. 'You had the ability, the university degree, and the opportunities others would have given their eye-teeth to possess!'

'Specifically . . . you?'

'Yes! I'm not ashamed to admit I would have given anything to have had it as easy as you did. I've had to achieve my ambition the hard way—working during the day and studying at night—whereas you . . . You had it all at your feet and wouldn't put it to use! All you wanted to do was generally enjoy the good life, be the playboy, go fishing. Although not necessarily in that order, naturally!' Her voice became laden with unbridled sarcasm.

'That's right! Because I had a singular lack of

interest in the work I *was* expected to do,' Dare shot back in an equally caustic vein. 'Because as much as it may surprise you, some of us do actually favour working closer to nature, do have a definite fancy to evade spending our whole working lives cloistered in cheerless steel and concrete office towers!'

'Although not to escape altogether the advantages Tremaynes can provide, I note!' Teal derided uncontrollably, sweeping a hand wide to indicate their surroundings.

Dare's features stilled. 'Meaning?'

'That it was quite acceptable for Tremaynes to finance this venture.'

'Except that there doesn't happen to be a cent of Tremayne Industries' money in Calanda,' she was informed in chafingly sardonic accents. 'The only funds invested here are my own, and what I've raised . . . independently.'

'Oh!' Teal chewed at her lip discomfitedly. Then, recovering her composure a little, she tenaciously returned to the attack, purring sweetly, 'The Tremayne name having absolutely no bearing on the success of that, I suppose.'

Thrusting his hands into the back pockets of his jeans, Dare regarded her lazily. 'Uh-uh, wrong again, my pet,' he drawled in veto. 'Names carry little weight with financial institutions unless they're backed by cold, hard facts such as market research, feasibility studies, projected profit margins, et cetera.' Pausing, he cast her a searching look. 'In any event, why should it matter to you, anyway?'

Teal shifted restively, hunching a deprecating

shoulder in reply as her feelings abruptly subsided
once more. Indeed, why *did* it matter to her? she
wondered. It was almost as if she had wanted to prove
he wasn't capable of making it on his own. But for
what reason? In retaliation for his having denounced
her own attitudes?

But surely the confirmation that their attitudes were
so different—if she had actually ever needed such
verification—should have been gratifying to her, not
stirring her into losing control . . . yet again, damn it!
Just when was she going to stop permitting herself to
be provoked into disputes relating to the past, and
concentrate on her work only instead? She decided
there was no time like the present.

'You still will be interfacing with Tremaynes'
mainframe, I assume,' she surmised, keeping her
voice as cool and calm as possible.

'If you mean by that, connecting our computer
system with theirs, then the answer is no,' Dare
contradicted. And, on seeing her surprised
expression, he shook his head wryly as he mocked,
'You do appear to be finding it inordinately difficult
to come to terms with the idea that this is a wholly
unaffiliated operation, don't you, precious?'

Teal's cheeks became tinged with rose. However,
she did manage to clamp down on her first
inclination, which was to remonstrate once more over
his aggravating choice of terminology. She more than
suspected it wouldn't have had any effect, in any case.

'I—well, with it being in the same family, we just
thought interfacing would be a matter of course, that's
all,' she explained, if somewhat stiltedly. Certainly

Dennis was going to be disappointed when he
discovered there was no such intention, the
involuntary thought ensued. She knew he had been
hoping for that much, at least.

'Thereby bringing ICS to the notice of Tremayne
Industries?' hazarded Dare shrewdly, beginning to
usher her along the downward-inclining path once
more.

Teal eased her tongue across dry lips. However,
guessing he had already come to his own
conclusion—Dare had always been quick-witted, if
nothing else—she followed her first nervous reaction
with a dismissive shrug. 'There's no harm in hoping,'
she declared on a faintly defiant note, and he cast her a
long, jaundiced look.

'That also being the reason Elford nominated you
for this project?' he demanded, his mouth shaping
cynically. 'Because he was hoping—because of your
previous association—that you might be able to exert
some influence in that regard?'

'No!' Teal protested immediately, and not a little
indignantly. 'Dennis would never do anything so
unprofessional. Besides, as I understand it, he'd
already advised you that I was to do your
programming before he was even aware I did know
you.' And so much, it would seem, for her speculation
that she might perhaps have been the reason Dare had
approached ICS in the first place!

'Although he was aware, of course, that you'd once
worked for Tremayne Industries.'

'The information's on record in my file, yes.
Although it wasn't until afterwards that he

remembered.' The qualification was swiftly added.

Dare's mouth quirked. 'That being *after* you had objected to being assigned the task, hmm?' he surmised drily, and all too astutely for Teal's liking, and her chin set at a defensively challenging level in consequence.

'So what makes you think I did protest?' she countered with what she hoped was just the right amount of scornful amusement.

The upward tilt to Dare's lips became more pronounced, the dappled light filtering through the clump of trees they were passing turning his thickly lashed eyes to a warm, beguiling topaz. 'Just the fact that every reference to the past has made you as uneasy as hell ever since you arrived,' he drawled eloquently.

Fighting frantically against the traitorous attraction his expression had abruptly induced, Teal drew a ragged breath. 'Because I've no wish to be reminded of it, that's why!'

'In case it destroys the cosy misconceptions you've created for yourself?'

She came to a gasping halt. 'What misconceptions?'

Dare moved a step closer, a strong, tanned hand reaching up to cup her chin, and causing her deep blue eyes to widen warily. 'For a start, the assumption that you could escape scot-free with regard to your own decidedly questionable actions,' he enlightened her a touch sardonically, and without warning he claimed her mouth with a possessive, demanding insistence that trapped her breath in her throat.

Shock held Teal frozen. Shock engendered by the

suddenly appalling knowledge that it seemed as if it had only been yesterday since he had last kissed her . . . *and* that she still liked the feel of his lips against hers as much as she ever had! No, it was unthinkable, her mind immediately rebelled in panicking denial. How could she still find anything pleasurable in his kiss after all the heartbreak he had caused her?

Then, just as abruptly as he had lowered his mouth to hers, Dare now raised his head again. 'You owed me that . . . for the way in which you left,' he declared with an indolently taunting smile.

Teal's face flamed—not only with humiliation because they were both aware she had made no attempt to break free, but also because his demeanour made it evident that the contact that had so disturbed her had affected him not at all—except for having provided an obviously satisfying retaliation.

'I owed you nothing, you bastard!' she choked in a mixture of rage and anguish. 'I was the one with reason to be aggrieved, not you.' She glared at him balefully.

Dare's expression assumed a sceptical aspect. 'On that point, it appears we differ.'

'We differ on all points!' Teal had no hesitation in amending in stony accents.

'Well, not quite all,' he contradicted in a wry murmur, his gaze travelling to her mouth and lingering there, explicitly, so that her face coloured helplessly once more. 'And who knows? Perhaps we'll discover other compatible areas while we're dining this evening.'

'Dining this evening?' Teal echoed with a stunned

gasp. She shook her head violently in negation. 'I have no intention of having dinner with you, either this or any other evening, Dare. Nor, might I add, do I have the slightest interest in finding any compatibility with you in anything except work-related fields. I'm here solely on business, and that's precisely how I mean it to continue.' She nodded emphatically to stress her point.

'And the restaurant trade *is* very much part of the farm's business,' came the smoothly voiced advice.

Teal touched her teeth indecisively to her lower lip. Yes, she supposed restaurants would constitute a good deal of their trade. Simultaneously, though, the rallying thought followed . . .

'But dining in one is somewhat incidental to any computer programming necessary, wouldn't you say?' She eyed him not a little triumphantly.

Dare's return gaze was equally complacent. 'I was under the impression that that was one of the reasons we hired you . . . to *professionally* analyse all facets of and everything connected with the whole operation, in order to give us the benefit of your expertise in recognising those areas that could provide useful data, or a more streamlined method of evaluating it, in case we may have overlooked something.' His muscled shoulders rose in a deprecating gesture. 'However, if Elford condones hit-or-miss judgements based on purely emotional grounds . . .'

'Dennis does not condone anything of the kind!' interrupted Teal vexedly in defence. His mention of the other man did prove timely, nevertheless. It reminded her, albeit somewhat guiltily, of Dennis's wish for this project, in particular, to be perfect from start to finish. Something that really couldn't have been said of it so far! Moreover, despite his original hopes concerning Tremayne having been dashed, he still wouldn't expect her to treat the work lightly, and nor would he understand her permitting herself to be sidetracked by emotional issues. He certainly never was. But he had made a point of reliability and thoroughness, she recalled. Expelling a heavy sigh, she sent Dare a cool and level look. 'And neither am I in the habit of making emotional, haphazard decisions,' she denied. 'If you'd bothered to explain properly, instead of making it sound as if it was only for—for social reasons . . .' Her lips compressed censuringly.

'If you hadn't immediately rushed to form another of your misconceptions . . .' He cast her a chafingly meaningful look.

Teal flushed and averted her gaze. The implication was that she shouldn't assume he was any more interested in becoming personally involved with her again than she was with him, she supposed, and she was embarrassed by the realisation that she had given the impression she believed otherwise. And all because he had kissed her—in retaliation, at that!—came the increasingly discomfiting thought. Would she never learn that Dare Tremayne was not to be taken seriously . . . *ever*?

'Yes—well, even though I still find it difficult to imagine just what data could possibly be obtained from such a source that would have any great relevance to your programming requirements,' inserted with purposeful deliberation, 'all right, I—I accept that I may have been a little hasty,' she granted reluctantly. Then, having got that out of the way, she went on, in more positive tones, 'None the less, should you have any further such—after-hours diversions planned for the future, I would appreciate some prior warning so that I can ensure I'm available. I wouldn't want you to think I wasn't giving your work due consideration by having to decline.' She allowed herself the satisfaction of a sweetly mocking smile.

Dare's lips twisted. 'Your social calendar that full, eh?'

She executed the smallest of deprecating shrugs. 'It's a long time since I've lived at home in Launceston, and I have a lot of friends there.'

'Male friends?'

Her jaw lifted minimally. 'Some.'

'That Elford's prepared to share you with?' He crooked a satirically incredulous brow.

Teal drew a deep breath. 'Sharing doesn't come into it!' she retorted. 'I said they were friends, nothing else. I'm glad to say two-timing doesn't happen to be something *I* practise!' An ungovernable thread of bitterness crept into her voice.

'Implying?' probed Dare, angling her a sidelong glance.

As if he didn't know, the perfidious, conscienceless reptile! Fury had Teal's blood close to boiling, but at the same time she was damned if she was going to give him the satisfaction of knowing that, even after all this time, annoyingly the thought of his infidelity still had the power to hurt unbearably.

'Only that I'm completely honest with Dennis in every regard,' she replied with careful calm, if between strongly gritted teeth. 'Because ours is a relationship based on mutual respect and trust, I'm glad to say.'

A muscle rippled at the side of Dare's jaw. 'Implying that you won't be cutting and running on him?' he derided with unexpected savagery.

Teal clamped her lips together to refrain from answering as her feelings dictated. Instead she concentrated, with no little satisfaction, on the speculation that she seemed to have struck a nerve, after all, with her last comment. It enabled her to face him with her mouth relaxing into a provoking smile.

'Oh, I shouldn't think so,' she said limpidly. 'Dennis is a man for a lasting relationship, not a casual affair.' She paused, her brows arching tauntingly. 'If you catch my drift.' She resumed walking before he had a chance to reply.

To Teal's relief, the rest of the day had passed a little more easily. She had seen over the remainder of the complex, and met both Laurie and Martha Debenham, a pleasant couple in their forties, with whom she and Dare had shared lunch in their comfortable home. As well, she had also been introduced to the farm's much younger trainee manager, and the two other male employees.

Consequently, as she dressed for dinner with Dare that evening, she was able to view the hours ahead with more composure than when he had first

mentioned it. After their last verbal skirmish she had
determined that the best attitude to adopt was that of
their involvement having been of little moment to her,
no matter how difficult that might be to portray, and
to try to keep up a distracting flow of conversation.
And in that regard, any conversation, even if related
to the past—although not to them directly, of
course—would have to be considered suitable, she
supposed grudgingly. Just so long as she ensured that
she retained control of the subject, and not Dare.

Now, on hearing a smoothly purring engine halt
outside, Teal gave her appearance a last check in the
mirror, applied a light spray of delicately scented
perfume, and made her way towards the front door in
time to see Dare being welcomed cordially into the
living-room by her parents.

Dressed in a dark and superbly fitting suit, his
tanned skin contrasting sharply with his white shirt,
his tawny eyes reflecting that reckless vitality that was
so much a part of him, he appeared confident and at
ease . . . and so similar to when Teal had originally
met him that her chest constricted, momentarily
leaving her breathless.

'Hmm . . . now that I like,' he approved in resonant
tones, leisurely surveying her sleeveless dress of dusky
pink and silver corded silk that traced the outline of
her curving figure so flatteringly.

Teal swallowed and inclined her head. That lazy,
warmly sensuous look he got in his eyes sometimes
had always been able to turn her stomach topsy-turvy.
'Thank you,' she just managed to push out, shakily.

'Then, if you're ready . . .' Dare stepped back a pace

to allow her room to precede him before turning to bid her parents goodnight.

'Oh, and I'll leave a pot of coffee heating for when you return,' said Mrs Hayworth with a smile, after her daughter had added her own words of farewell. 'I expect Dare would like a cup before heading back to the farm.'

Teal's heart sank but, even as she despaired of her parent's sense of hospitality, she had little choice but to nod a weak concurrence. In truth, she hadn't even been intending to invite Dare past the front gate on their return.

Dare's car, a sleek and shining black Porsche, was parked in the driveway, and as she slid on to the dark red leather seat Teal was startled by the feeling of complete familiarity, of a disturbing rightness in her being there, that immediately assailed her. It was just as if she could open the glove compartment and discover her belongings there, just as they had been before, and she found the experience distinctly unnerving.

'Is this the same car you used to drive?' she asked somewhat jerkily, almost accusingly, as soon as Dare had taken the seat beside her.

Switching on the ignition, he slanted her a faintly amused look at her tone. 'Is there any reason why it shouldn't be?' he countered wryly.

Teal sucked in a steadying breath and shook her head. Whatever was the matter with her? It was stupid to allow a mere car to have such an effect on her. 'No, of course not,' she denied, endeavouring to make her voice sound as mirthful as his had. 'When I first saw it

I—I just assumed you'd updated, that's all.'

Dare shrugged and began reversing. 'There was no call to. This one suits me fine. Besides . . .' he brought them to a halt before swinging on to the roadway, his mouth curving into a wide smile that made Teal's pulse race, 'for the last few years my greatest need has been equipment for the farm rather than a new car.'

Flustered, she could only manage a limp nod of understanding, and was glad when he turned away to set the vehicle moving again. 'So—so just when did you actually start the farm?' she enquired after a few moments, her curiosity finally getting the better of her.

'Just five years ago,' he told her without taking his eyes from the road as he headed them into the city. 'Although it's only been for the last three that we've really been in production, of course. It takes time, but thank heavens, it's all beginning to pay off now.'

So he must have started it very shortly after she had left, Teal mused, and couldn't help wondering if he had had it in mind while they were still together, and why he hadn't said so, if that had been the case. But that wasn't a question she could ask, of course. That was too close to what she least wanted to resurrect.

'Your father must have been very disappointed when you left Tremaynes, though,' she hazarded tentatively instead.

The corner of Dare's mouth that she could see crooked ruefully. 'Yes and no.' There was a brief pause, and he spared her a glance that had turned derisively acid. 'Although he was at least a damn sight more understanding than you ever were!'

Resentment bubbled, but with an iron effort of will she succeeded in only allowing an edge of mockery to accent her tone as she gibed, 'You call the arguments you and he used to have . . . understanding?'

'Regardless, he was still prepared to acknowledge that I had ambitions of my own . . . as distinct from his!'

'Oh?' There was a wealth of disbelief in the exclamation. He had never mentioned anything of the kind to her. 'To start a fish farm?'

Dare's lips twisted. 'Not necessarily. As surprising as you may find it, I wanted the challenge of making it on my own . . . not merely stepping into someone else's shoes!' He released an audible breath. 'I tried it that way, and it didn't work.'

'Not that I can recall you ever trying particularly hard,' Teal couldn't forbear from sniping.

'And since you were only with the company during the last few months of the three *years* I was there, you wouldn't really know,' he returned disparagingly, and his words stung.

'Then why didn't you ever say anything about it to me?' she flared. 'Why give the impression that the only things of importance to you were going fishing and—and generally having a good time?'

Dare uttered a short, not altogether mirthful, half-laugh. 'Because fishing, especially, was important to me. I'd always been interested in everything concerning trout.' He flicked her a dour glance. 'While as for confiding in you . . . there didn't seem any point. You always made it more than evident you couldn't see past the supposed advantages to be gained by meekly following in my father's footsteps.'

Teal's eyes flashed with sparks of indignation. 'Then if my attitude was so shockingly repellent to you, I'm surprised you weren't the one to end our—our association,' she flung at him tartly.

Coming to a stop at a set of traffic lights, Dare slanted her a sardonic gaze. 'Yeah, well, I did wonder that myself, but I guess we're all permitted one mistake in our lives.' He paused. 'Besides, there were other . . . compensations.' His eyes ranged insolently, explicitly, over her body.

Hot, mortified colour promptly swept into Teal's face, and her hands clenched tightly in her lap. Nevertheless, even as her humiliated feelings demanded a retaliatory response, her brain protectively advocated otherwise. She couldn't let him know their affair had meant more to her than it had to him, the frantic warning kept pounding in her head. She just couldn't!

'Yes, at least in that regard I suppose our relationship did provide *some* satisfying moments,' she granted at length in as detached and bored a voice as she could contrive, then continued hurriedly in a, she hoped, diverting manoeuvre, 'So you have no connection, in any shape or form, with Tremayne Industries now, I gather.'

Momentarily, Dare regarded her speculatively, then gave an impassive flexing of a broad shoulder as the lights turned green and they began moving again. 'No, I still have some input. It does remain basically a family concern, after all.' His brows drew together thoughtfully. 'In fact, there's a family business meeting scheduled for Thursday evening.' A corner of his well-shaped mouth started to lift. 'Perhaps you'd better accompany me to it,' he proposed unexpectedly, and Teal frowned.

'Me? Whatever for?' she questioned half-incredulously, half suspiciously.

'Why not? You've met them all before, and you may find it interesting. In any case, I'm sure they'd be pleased to see you again.'

Teal couldn't imagine why, and shook her head confusedly. Just what was behind this? Only minutes ago he had been witheringly deprecating. 'Dare, you said yourself, it's a *family* business meeting . . .' She inhaled deeply. 'I don't think it's a good idea for . . .'

'I suspect Elford would disagree,' he interjected smoothly.

'Dennis?' she echoed, totally perplexed now. 'What has he to do with it?'

'Well, you did say he was hoping for ICS to be brought to Tremaynes' notice, didn't you? So where better to do that than at such a meeting?'

Teal's brows flew skywards. He had made the suggestion on Dennis's behalf? She couldn't believe it and, as a result, she temporised, 'Except that I rather think it was our work he was hoping to have brought to their attention, not one of his staff.'

Dare shrugged. 'Meaning, you're declining the opportunity?'

'I didn't say that exactly,' she denied swiftly. Even if there was only the merest chance of it generating some work for them, Dennis would still never forgive her if she didn't accept it, she surmised. 'It's just that . . .' She broke off with a helpless sigh, her lips compressing. 'The meeting's on Thursday, you said . . .?'

CHAPTER FOUR

THE RESTAURANT was relatively new, but already becoming recognised as one of the city's finest. Situated over looking the Tamar River, it was known not only for its splendidly scenic location, but even more for the quality of its food and wines—and its rapidly growing popularity. The latter was much in evidence this evening, Teal noted, and giving her cause to eye her companion quizzically as soon as they were seated at their table.

'You must have been very fortunate in managing to obtain a table here tonight on such short notice,' she began musingly, scanning the already almost-full room. 'Or was it already booked?'

Dare shook his head, smiling, but the appearance of a waiter to take their order for aperitifs deferred any elaboration until after their order had been given and the man departed.

'No, Gareth—Gareth Maunder, the owner—is an old friend from way back, and since I helped promote the restaurant when he first started, he always makes a table available whenever I want one,' he explained. 'In return, I ensure that he never receives anything but the absolute best of the trout into his kitchen.'

Teal's expression became bantering. 'You mean they don't all fit into that category?'

Dare laughed, a low, vibrant sound that stirred the

senses. 'No, even under controlled conditions, they still produce superior specimens, exactly the same as every other living organism does. How else could we keep upgrading our breeding stock if they didn't?'

'Oh, you don't breed from all of them, then?'

'Uh-uh! Only from the pick of the species' representatives. In any case, with each female producing in the vicinity of five thousand eggs, and with an over ninety per cent fertilisation rate on the farm, we would very shortly be swamped with more fish—as well as of a lesser quality—than we could possibly handle.'

Teal nodded. 'And how long does it take for them to reach marketable size?'

'About eighteen months. They weigh some three hundred grams—or three-quarters of a pound—by then,' Dare advised briefly as the owner himself arrived at the table carrying an ice-bucket and their champagne.

Of much the same age as Dare, although shorter and less muscular, Gareth greeted his friend with a welcoming smile and, with the introductions completed and the wine poured, remained to talk.

'I'm glad you came in tonight. There's something I wanted to have a word with you about,' he said to Dare. To Teal, with an apologetic look, he requested, 'You'll excuse me if I engage him in business for just a minute?'

Lowering her glass, Teal spread a hand wide in invitation. 'Go right ahead,' she urged equably with a smile. 'Business is the reason we're here.'

'Oh?' He glanced from one to the other of them in

obvious surprise.

As well he might, mused Teal wryly. After all, the bottle resting in the bucket beside the table was usually associated with celebrations rather than mere business. But then, as a Tremayne, Dare always had been in a position to entertain nothing but the very best, came the ensuing thought as she listened to him explaining their circumstances to the other man.

Presently, with the arrival of another waiter bearing the menu, Gareth took his departure, and as she ran her eye down the list of dishes Teal couldn't contain the half-laugh that rose to her lips. As a result of the champagne on an empty stomach, she suspected.

'I don't suppose I'd better choose anything other than the trout, had I?' she quizzed.

Dare's regard turned lazy. 'That's up to you,' he allowed easily. 'If you would prefer something else . . .'

Teal shook her head. 'No, I'll have the trout.' She paused, her lingering smile widening. 'If only to prove I haven't forgotten your advice on how to remove all the flesh from the bones in two easy movements.' She proceeded to quote, 'Above the lateral line, or backbone, vertically towards the dorsal fin; below the lateral line, at a forty-five-degree angle towards the tail.'

Dare quirked a whimsical brow. 'So you didn't find absolutely everything from those days entirely forgettable?' he drawled wryly.

Teal caught at her lower lip with even white teeth. Forgettable? After all the years she had spent trying to put it out of her mind? 'No, not absolutely everything,' she granted in a low, uneven voice, and swiftly returned her attention to the menu.

By the time they had given their orders and their avocado pears had arrived, Teal had recovered her composure—helped considerably, she had to admit, by Dare not pursuing his previous disconcerting line of thought. Consequently, as she spooned her way through the appetising green flesh, she was able to feel more comfortable again.

'So what did you think of Gareth's suggestion?' enquired Dare interestedly at one point, and she felt strangely flattered that he should even give any consideration to her opinion.

'About you providing much larger, single fish suitable for a whole table of diners?' Her head tilted thoughtfully. 'Well, that banquet-style of eating is becoming very popular nowadays, so I guess I would have to say it sounds like a good idea . . . provided it doesn't present you with any problems in growing the fish to that size.'

Dare discounted that possibility with a negative move of his head. 'No, as long as we can be certain of the numbers likely to be required, that shouldn't create any problems. It simply means we retain a proportion of them longer, that's all.'

'While at the same time, perhaps encouraging other restaurants to consider the idea too, if you advise them you'll have such fish available in future,' put in Teal consideringly. 'After all, keeping your clients up to date on these matters will be effortless once your computer's operating. Sorting out which letter goes to whom, and inserting the relevant names and addresses, et cetera, is one of the functions they perform best, and most easily. Unlike typists, they thrive on repetition,' she added with an expressive laugh.

'Something Martha will be thrilled to hear, I've no doubt,' he remarked drily.

'She normally does your typing?'

'Or I.' His accompanying grimace was so rueful that she grinned widely.

'While I'm here, I'll teach you to type properly, if you like,' she suddenly found herself offering impulsively.

'You reckon that's possible?'

Teal took a sip of her champagne and sent him a chaffing look above the rim of the glass. 'I guess that all depends on which one of us you're insinuating is incapable.'

Dare smiled slowly, his eyes assuming a sleepy look as he viewed her, and particularly her mouth, from between half-closed lids. 'Or which of us is likely to admit defeat first,' he countered in a soft drawl.

The steady beat of Teal's heart stumbled, and she gulped another mouthful of her drink. Had there been a subtle change of direction in that remark, or was it just the wine making her imagine it? she speculated.

'As to that, I suppose only time will tell,' she replied in as lightly unconcerned a tone as she could manage.

Dare inclined his head indolently. 'I guess it will,' was his only comment, to her relief, before he went on to talk about something else.

It was only towards the end of their meal that Teal experienced any further disconcerting moments—

although in a manner she simply hadn't anticipated, and causing her considerable consternation as a result.

The first time, there was only a niggling sense of indignation when they were interrupted by a vivacious blonde who was making her way to her own table along with her escort.

'Hi! Long time no see,' she greeted Dare brightly, stroking a carmine-tipped hand familiarly across his shoulder. 'We must get together again some time . . . OK?' She smiled at him invitingly over her shoulder as she continued on her way.

However, as far as Teal was concerned, it was their second such interruption that created her most alarming inner turmoil. On this occasion it was a svelte and elegantly attired brunette who crossed to their table while her own companion attended to the bill.

'Dare!' she began on a huskily sensuous note, making his name sound like a caress. 'Why haven't you called? I've been back in town for almost two weeks now.' Her full red lips pouted prettily in reproach. 'Give me a ring tomorrow and we'll arrange to celebrate my return . . . just the two of us . . . at my place,' she continued with unmistakable meaning, and Teal felt her every emotion flare in unexpected protest.

And not simply with resentment for the woman's sheer hide in attempting to make such an assignation in front of Dare's present dinner partner, she realised in shocked alarm. There was a certain antagonism, an invidiously outraged sense of possession, there as well. So what did she care how many females he wined, dined and/or bedded? she told herself hastily. Hadn't she remarked only that morning that a lack of women willing to keep him company had never been one of Dare's problems? Luckily, the thought proved bolstering, so that when the brunette's escort reached her, and they departed, she could exhibit a mocking amusement when she met Dare's gaze.

'I'm sorry if I'm cramping your style, but . . . how awkward for you to have such—er—close friends here tonight . . . and both so eager to help you while away your leisure hours too,' she purred.

Dare leant back idly in his chair. 'Neither of which offer do I have any intention of availing myself, none the less,' he advised, drily matter-of-fact.

Teal ventured a glance from beneath long, curling lashes. 'Another two bitten the dust, as it were, hmm?' She clicked her tongue chidingly. 'You'll run out of new prospects if you're not careful.'

'And maybe I'm not looking for any new prospects.'

'Got enough others to keep you going for the present, have you?'

'Could be,' he wasn't averse to allowing in a laconic drawl. His head tilted and he crooked an expressive brow. 'Any particular reason you're apparently so singularly interested?'

Teal swallowed, but managed to force a reasonably dismissive laugh. 'Oh, no, not interested,' she disputed. 'Simply grateful I'm not one of their number any more.'

'You never were,' asserted Dare levelly, and her breathing quickened.

Oh, yes, he would allege that, wouldn't he? He

doubtless said the same to all his female companions. But she knew better, of course!

'Yes—well, that's all water under the bridge now, in any case. These days I prefer less—turbulent relationships,' she returned with some asperity.

Dare's mouth turned up a little at one corner. 'Including an absence of the fiery passions we also aroused in each other?' he hazarded on a subtle note.

His evocative words had Teal's heartbeat accelerating wildly as, for the second time that day, they brought long-denied memories waywardly flooding back into her mind. Recollections so vivid, so intense that even now they had the power to send waves of fire coursing to her every extremity, and to make her limbs tremble.

'I—I hardly think that's a suitable topic for the dinner-table,' she evaded on a slightly strangled note.

Dare gave a faint shrug. 'Then, if you've finished, shall we go?'

Teal's stomach constricted, her gaze turning wary, but since she had already had two cups of coffee and really didn't want a third she could only nod weakly. At least the sooner she returned home, the sooner she would be relieved of his disconcerting presence, she consoled herself.

On arriving at the house, Teal left Dare to make himself at home in the living-room while she bustled about in the kitchen, adding the coffee to the tray her mother had left set for them. Not that she, for one, was the least interested in drinking any of it. The more so since it would only serve to prolong Dare's departure.

On her return to the living-room she found Dare seated on the sofa, his jacket removed, and his tie and the top buttons of his shirt loosened. He looked totally relaxed and at ease, his presence so vital, so overpoweringly masculine, that she somehow felt crowded, as if the room had suddenly shrunk in size. He made it feel as if it was his home, not hers! she thought resentfully as she set the tray on the low table in front of the sofa and seated herself in an armchair opposite.

'Just sugar?' Her enquiry was made a trifle snappishly after she had poured some coffee into one of the cups.

'You remembered?' Dare arched a mockingly provoking brow.

'I noticed in the restaurant,' Teal took pleasure in correcting with a chafing smile as she handed him the cup.

His lips twisted. 'So your memory hasn't really improved, then?'

'Meaning?'

'When I arrived earlier, your mother just happened to ask in passing if you'd given me their regards this morning . . . as requested,' he relayed in an expressive drawl.

Teal's eyes widened in remembrance, and she shifted uncomfortably in her seat. 'I'm sorry—it slipped my mind,' she apologised grudgingly. Then, in an accusing vein, 'If you hadn't kept introducing so many irrelevant issues of a personal nature, I would probably have remembered.'

'Mention of the past—distracts you, does it?'

Teal inhaled deeply. 'When I'm only interested in my present work, yes, I suppose you could say that,' she averred tartly.

Dare digested her retort in silence, drinking his coffee, and then eyeing the other empty cup on the tray. 'You're not joining me?'

Teal shook her head. 'No, I'm afraid it tends to keep me awake if I have coffee too late at night,' she prevaricated.

'It didn't used to.'

Damn him for remembering! 'Well, it does now, obviously!' she continued to assert on a guiltily flaring note.

'If you say so,' he allowed in such a smooth voice that she knew immediately he didn't believe a word of it, and she couldn't suppress the flush that promptly stained her cheeks. After a brief glance towards the hallway, he went on in a more conversational tone, 'Your parents gone to bed already, have they?'

She only wished they hadn't! 'Yes, they're leaving very early in the morning to go fishing for the day,' she told him.

Dare's mouth shaped eloquently. 'Half their luck!' Pausing, he slanted her an infuriating glance, his tawny eyes gleaming. 'So your mother has no objections to the pastime, then?'

Implying, as she'd had where he was concerned, Teal deduced, her own eyes flashing blue sparks. 'More than likely because Dad didn't devote himself to it until he'd retired from work . . . not the other way round!' she rejoined snidely.

An impenitent laugh issued from Dare's bronzed throat. 'Those claws of yours are on show again, my pet,' he reproved lazily, depositing his cup on the table.

Teal dipped her head tauntingly. 'When you're involved, it just seems to come naturally,' she quipped with a deceptively sweet smile.

'Mmm—surprisingly, one might say, in view of your repeated claims about the past not being important to you, and you having forgotten all about it, et cetera.' He fixed her with an all too perceptive glance as he rose leisurely.

Teal sprang to her own feet somewhat more jerkily, taking a deep breath to still the sudden wild beating of her heart. 'Unless, of course, someone else refuses to allow it to remain dead and buried,' she just managed to get out pointedly.

'Even if, as it would appear, only shallowly.' His accompanying smile was as smooth as his voice.

She forced a dismissive shrug. 'Or that's what your ego would apparently like to believe, anyway,' she gibed over her shoulder as she made for the doorway to ensure his departure.

Donning his jacket, Dare followed her at a casual pace. 'Or rather, *you* would prefer to think that was the only reason,' he countered in a drily mocking drawl.

The tip of Teal's tongue circled her lips. 'You're crazy!' she threw at him flusteredly, and swiftly turned into the hall.

'Am I?' Strong fingers caught at her shoulder,

compelling her back against the wall. 'Perhaps I know you better than you think, my pet.'

Trapped between the hands that now rested against that same wall on either side of her head, Teal felt the pulse in her throat quicken, her whole body suddenly seeming to become treacherously attuned to the hard muscularity of his as he leant into her.

'Or—or you've mistakenly convinced yourself you do,' she contradicted unsteadily, a little breathlessly.

A slow smile—heart-catching, mesmerising— touched the corners of Dare's lips. 'You think so?' he murmured quietly, his head lowering to hers.

He meant to kiss her again, Teal realised abruptly in some consternation, but although her mind framed words of protest her mouth waywardly refused to give voice to them. Appallingly, it seemed more interested in savouring the feel and taste of his as it took possession of her lips with such persuasive leisurely skill.

And why wouldn't he be skilled? He wasn't exactly unpractised! came the immediate, scornful thought . . . but to no avail. Her body seemed to have developed a will of its own. One which drew her to him in spite of everything that had gone before, and which finally had her surrendering helplessly to the sensuous demands of his warm mouth . . . just as she had in the past.

Slowly, Dare drew her lower lip between his own, his tongue gliding over the sensitive inner flesh lingeringly, tantalisingly, and then penetrating further to search out the soft depths, to languidly possess, until her lips were clinging unreservedly to his and her tongue entangling wantonly with his own.

Feelings she could neither dispel nor deny—of excitement, a stirring of desire—raced through her, and, shocked and shaken by the devastating realisation, she at last tore her mouth free with a breathless gasp. It stunned her to think how willingly she had acquiesced, but worse, how easily he had been able to arouse emotions she had long believed dead—at least where he was concerned.

'I—I don't know what that was supposed to prove,' she pushed out shakily, but steadfastly doing her best to hold Dare's darkened gaze with eyes that were unknowingly wary, deep blue smudges in the paleness of her strained features.

Removing a hand from the wall, where they had remained the whole time—he hadn't even had to hold her to have her submitting! Teal lamented—Dare brushed a finger slowly across her still damp lower lip. And she felt too paralysed to stop him.

'I guess, when you're involved, it just seems to come naturally,' he said softly, using her own earlier claim, but when Teal felt an aching sensation within in response she shook her head violently in rejection.

'Then I suggest it doesn't again in future,' she recommended in huskily taut accents. 'As I've said before, whatever was between us is long gone, and any attempt to pretend otherwise is merely a waste of both my time and yours.'

Dare shook his head in negation. 'Liar,' he denounced quietly with gentle mockery. 'That was no pretence, and we both know it.' Before she could

ascertain his intent, he bent his head to graze her
mouth with his own once more. 'Nor, might I add,
would I ever consider kissing you a waste of time.'
With a crooked half-smile playing about his lips, he
turned for the front door, only pausing briefly after
opening it to look back to where she was still slumped
numbly against the wall. 'Sleep on it . . . and I'll see
you in the morning,' he proposed lazily before
disappearing through the opening.

Not until the door had shut behind him did Teal
move, and then merely to rest her head back against
the wall in an anguished gesture, her eyes closing in
despair.

You bloody fool! she castigated unsparingly with a
sob of self-disgust. You're letting him get to you all
over again!

The following morning Teal arrived at the farm in a
possibly more apprehensive state of mind than she
had the day before, but on driving around to the
office, where a desk had been made available for her,
she was relieved to discover a note saying that Dare
was down at the hatchery. It provided her with just
that little extra time to settle in and prepare herself for
their next meeting. With luck, she might even be so
involved in her work that she could only spare him
the briefest of greetings.

However, before she had even finished extracting
from her briefcase the notes she had made the
previous day, together with some other relevant
paperwork, the phone rang and she crossed to Dare's
desk to answer it.

'There's a call for you,' said a somewhat aggressive voice which she recognised as Amy's, and before she even had time to make an acknowledgement there was a click and another female voice sounded in her ear.

'Teal? Have we actually managed to contact you at last?'

Teal grimaced into the mouthpiece. 'It's still only eight-thirty, Claudia,' she pointed out drily, wondering why it should have been that girl, in particular, ringing her, anyway. 'How much earlier did you expect me to arrive?'

Claudia gave a tittering laugh. 'That's not for me to say, of course . . . but in view of you apparently getting along *so well* with the boss of the place that you *dined* together the very first night . . .' Her voice trailed off explicitly, and Teal gritted her teeth in vexation at the construction the other girl was attempting to put on the matter—and all for Dennis's benefit, most likely! 'Or didn't your mother pass on the message that we tried to ring you while you were out—*on the town?*'

Teal's fingers tightened involuntarily about the receiver. 'Yes, my mother left a note to say that *Dennis,*' stressed pointedly to gainsay the other girl's aggravating 'we', 'had tried to contact me,' she responded with something of a snap. She had found the message in her room when she'd gone to bed. 'I intended returning his call shortly.'

'Oh, you arrived home so *late* last night that your mother couldn't tell you *in person,*' put in Claudia in pseudo-innocent tones, and Teal's lips compressed wrathfully.

'Only because my parents went to bed earlier than usual,' she disclosed testily, reluctantly. It was no business of Claudia's, in any event!

'How very—opportune,' accompanied by a suggestive half-laugh. 'Especially since I hear you and Dare Tremayne weren't exactly—*strangers* to one another in the first place.'

Teal's breath caught in her throat. There was only one person who could have told Claudia that, and disappointment, coupled with a certain annoyance, hit her like a wave at the thought of Dennis having made such a revelation . . . and to Claudia, of all people! Or had it been the whole office? Regardless, Claudia would soon ensure that everyone was put in the picture, the depressing realisation swiftly followed.

'And our having met before . . .'

'Only—*met*? Oh, don't be so coy, Teal!' interposed the other girl with another grating laugh. 'At least be *honest* about it. Dennis and I don't hold it against you—*really*!'

Teal saw red. 'And I can't begin to tell you how ecstatic I am to hear that, Claudia!' she fired back with unbounded sarcasm. 'But now that you've so considerately put my mind at rest, would you kindly *get off the line,* and just put me through to Dennis?'

'Well, of course, if that's what you want,' Claudia acceded in plaintive accents, and Teal could almost see her pouting in supposed hurt. 'You don't have to take it out on *me* just because you've been—er—*caught out,* as it were. I'm sure we'll find your explanation *most* enlightening . . . if nothing else. Connecting you now,' she stated quickly, preventing Teal from responding, although only until she heard Dennis on the line, whereupon she launched immediately into censuring speech.

'Dennis! How could you have told Claudia about my relationship with Dare Tremayne? I didn't expect it to go beyond the two of us!' She paused to draw breath. 'And just for interest's sake, what's she doing making your phone calls for you, anyway?'

'Because she offered; young Belinda not having arrived as yet,' she was informed in an unexpectedly flat tone. 'As for the other . . . of course I didn't tell her.' A touch of indignation surfaced. 'What makes you think I did?'

Mollified somewhat by his answer, Teal calmed down sufficiently to quip, albeit sardonically, 'Mainly, the remarks she had to make a moment ago.' Then, with a frown, 'But if you didn't tell her, then who on earth did?'

'I wouldn't have any idea.' He seemed to hesitate momentarily. 'Unless . . .' There was another pause.

'Yes?' she prompted urgently.

'I—well, she was here when I tried to contact you last night, and I did happen to mention that the fact that you'd known Tremayne previously was partly the reason I was ringing,' he relayed thoughtfully. 'But that's all I said, so I doubt she could have guessed the rest from that.'

Teal's eyes sought the ceiling expressively. Only Dennis, with work preoccupying his mind to such a major extent, could be unsuspecting enough to think that. 'Well, what's done is done, I suppose,' she had little choice but to accept, even if with a disappointed sigh. As had already been proved, Claudia would have no compunction in using, or misusing, the information in any way possible for her own purposes. 'Although I'm not quite sure just why you had to tell her anything, or more importantly, why she was apparently with you when you made the call.' A trace of asperity edged into her tone.

'Because when I said I'd be working late, she kindly offered to remain behind to help,' Dennis revealed matter-of-factly, and Teal made a disgruntled *moue*. She didn't doubt Claudia would have positively leapt at the opportunity. 'As for mentioning the matter to her . . . well, that was only because she noticed I seemed—to her, at least—unnecessarily concerned about you.' He paused, and when he next spoke his voice had resumed its earlier flat intonation. 'And evidently she was correct, in view of your going out to dinner with Tremayne the very first evening after renewing your—acquaintanceship with him.'

Teal exhaled heavily. So that was at the bottom of his unusually spiritless manner . . . eagerly fostered by Claudia, of course! 'Except that my accompanying him was solely in connection with my work here, and for no other reason,' she was in the process of explaining decisively when, from the corner of her eye, she detected a movement and, turning her head, saw Dare leaning negligently against the door-frame.

The indolently knowing smile playing about his lips informed her immediately that he was well aware of who she was defending herself against, and why, and she couldn't control the self-conscious colour that stole into her cheeks before she swiftly turned her back to him. These definitely weren't the circumstances she had envisaged for their next meeting after last night's perturbing lapse of restraint on her part!

'Your work? In what way?' She suddenly realised Dennis was questioning but, no matter how she tried to concentrate on replying, the greatest part of her consciousness remained nervously centred on Dare's presence as she sensed rather than saw him approaching the desk.

'Well—er—naturally the restaurant trade forms a—a large part of the farm's custom,' she began with a stammer, then uttered a choked gasp as she felt Dare graze the exposed and sensitive nape of her neck with his mouth.

Wild sensations promptly sped down her spine, and she leapt agitatedly from her perch on the corner of the desk, knocking a pile of books and a pencil container to the floor with a noisy clatter as she did so.

'What in heaven's name is going on?' demanded Dennis a trifle tersely.

Struggling for composure, Teal cast Dare a baleful glare before faltering, 'Oh—um—I accidentally knocked some things off the desk.' Pausing, she deliberately looked straight at Dare as she added, 'There was an insect crawling on me.'

'Is that all?' Dennis sounded unimpressed, but it was Dare who retained Teal's attention, and she experienced a momentary tingle of precarious excitement on seeing his audaciously glinting amber eyes slant wickedly as he moved towards her. 'So, you were saying about the restaurant trade?' Dennis went on to prompt.

Teal didn't, couldn't, immediately answer. She was too occupied in both backing around the desk as far as the telephone cord allowed, and attempting to look her haughtiest at the same time. Hadn't she worn her most severely styled outfit in the hope of creating just such a stand-offish effect? Not that it appeared to be succeeding, and when the cord couldn't be stretched any further she was reduced to raising a repelling hand.

'Teal! Are you still there?' The tone of the voice in her ear was becoming a little impatient.

'Y-yes, of course,' she replied at last, jerkily, and almost dropped the receiver when Dare caught hold of her free hand to draw it to his mouth, his lips finding and lingering against the suddenly throbbing vein in her wrist.

'Stop that!' she mouthed at him in a panic as she felt her skin searing beneath his warm mouth, and vainly tried to wrench her hand free.

His response was merely to flash her a wide, rakish and utterly devastating smile, before turning his attention to her quivering fingers. The feel of his tongue stroking them sensuously as he took each of them into his mouth in turn had Teal staring at him helplessly, shocked into a state of suspended animation . . . except for her heart. That pounded so loudly that she was certain they both must have been able to hear it.

'*Teal!*' Sheer exasperation was evident in Dennis's voice now, but at least it succeeded in startling her back into life.

'Yes—yes, I'm here,' she gasped raggedly, doing her utmost to ignore the feelings Dare was arousing, and force herself to concentrate on Dennis instead. 'The restaurant trade . . . there are large numbers of fish involved . . . it could have provided necessary data . . . high-demand periods . . . sizes . . .' She broke off on a shuddering breath, unable to continue as Dare's mouth sucked at one of her fingers, tugging, releasing, making it impossible for her to even think straight, let alone speak coherently.

How could she when he was doing such electrifying things to her nervous system? Dear heaven, he always had known how to use his mouth to such tumultuous effect!

'I—I'm sorry, I have to—to go now,' she just managed to push out weakly, evasively, to Dennis. 'I'll ring you back as—as soon as I can.' She hung up hastily even as he started to remonstrate.

Immediately she did so, Dare released her hand, although only after touching his lips stirringly to her wrist again, and in an effort to repudiate the warm wave of aching feeling that rippled through her she sought denial in anger.

'Just what were you trying to do? Get me fired?' she demanded on a flaring but still somewhat breathless note.

Dare's lips twitched. 'Fire . . . his favourite girl?'

Teal angled her head higher. 'That's on a personal level. Where work's concerned, Dennis expects a professional manner.'

'Then maybe you should have considered that before mentioning insects,' he put forward in a drily amused drawl.

Teal bit her lip. 'I wouldn't have had to, if you hadn't kissed my neck first!' she defended.

Flexing a muscled shoulder, Dare seated himself casually on the edge of the desk. 'It was presented to me so enticingly, I simply couldn't help myself,' he excused with an unrepentant and beguiling smile that made a travesty of her efforts to gainsay his attraction.

'Well, you'd better ensure that you can in future!' she snapped irritably in consequence as she prepared to storm past him.

A blocking arm promptly barred her path, then swept her back to face him in an inescapable movement that brought her disconcertingly close to his rugged form, imprisoned between his long, outstretched legs.

'Why?' he quizzed not a little sardonically, his hands at her waist preventing any escape. 'Because you didn't like it, or merely because you think that's what you *ought* to say?'

Teal's breasts rose and fell rapidly, and she moistened her dry lips with the tip of her tongue. She tried to stand stiffly, her hands clenched at her sides, but that only put them in contact with the hard muscularity of Dare's thighs and she moved them swiftly, as if they had suddenly been burnt.

His proximity was nerve-racking, his careless masculinity overwhelming, making her feel flustered and vulnerable . . . and abruptly, intolerably, aware once again that far from her being able to dismiss him, her emotions were by no means indifferent to his presence.

'Because I'm not interested, of course!' she asserted agitatedly at length, and as much to impress the fact on herself as him. 'As you just pointed out, I'm Dennis's girl these days.'

'Mmm . . .' Dare's mouth shaped wryly as his ebony-framed eyes leisurely contemplated her changing expressions. 'But somehow I suspect he's not the all-consuming male in your life in return,' he speculated softly.

Teal swallowed hard. 'And you wouldn't know whether he was or not!' she disputed on a defensive note.

'Wouldn't I?' Suddenly his hands were framing her face, and the pupils of her deep blue eyes dilated nervously. 'I thought we'd gone through all this last night.'

'Except that you're no more correct now than . . .' Her frantic denial was cut off in mid-sentence, stifled by his possessive lips closing demandingly over hers.

Determined to remain unresponsive, Teal refused to struggle. She desperately wanted to prove, to herself as much as Dare, that she could control her emotions, and that her reaction the previous evening had merely been a brief lapse on her part, brought about by the mellow feeling of repletion induced by the rich food and wine she had consumed.

Nevertheless, as his mouth continued to move on hers, insistent, searching, his tongue outlining the fullness of her lower lip, to her horror she felt a hauntingly familiar ache beginning to spread through her, and a sob of trepidation rose in her throat. The next instant Dare's probing tongue was invading the moist recesses of her mouth, tasting them and claiming them as his own until she was lost in a maelstrom of reeling senses and naked needs that betrayed her last attempts at resistance.

Almost before she knew it, her fingers were tangling within his dark hair, her body melting against the length of his in a heated desire to know once more the feel of his hard, moulded muscles fitted so intimately to her own pliant curves. Dare uttered an indistinct sound of pleasure at the feel of her lissom body, his sinewed arms immediately pinning her tightly to him.

Now Teal's tongue actively sought his own, sparring with it, teasing it, her emotions lifted to fever pitch when he drew it between his lips to suck at it erotically, relinquish, tug again, just as he had done with her finger earlier. Then he was murmuring something against the corner of her mouth, his voice husky with emotion, the look in his eyes no less instense when he slowly, reluctantly, raised his head.

'No, my pet, Elford doesn't hold pride of place in your life,' he contended in rough and unexpectedly taut tones. Then, touching a finger to her parted lips, 'Nor is what was between us over.' Fleetingly, his mouth took the place of his finger. 'But this time . . . the ending's going to be on *my* terms.'

CHAPTER FIVE

WITH DARE'S eventual departure, Teal struggled for a return of equilibrium and a rational organisation of her thoughts.

Although forced to face the idea, no matter how alarming, that Dare might not have been altogether wrong in his claim that whatever had been between them wasn't as dead and buried as she had believed—how else could she explain those wayward feelings that kept sneaking up on her so ungovernably?—her mind, at least, still rebelled at the thought. Dear heaven, how many kinds of fool was she?

Couldn't she see that it was just a game to Dare? An amusing one, at that, undoubtedly! To have her succumbing again, merely to afford him the opportunity to dictate the terms of their parting this time, would provide the sweetest of revenge, wouldn't it? Or, put another way, he was simply playing her like he would one of his damn fish! One among many, too, more than likely, if the pair in the restaurant had been any guide . . . and just like before, the waspishly grimaced denunciation ensued.

Luckily, that thought proved to be one that seemed to lead by natural progression to another—that she had been right to put her work first then, and likewise, that there was no reason why that shouldn't also be her life-saver now. At least where work was concerned she was totally in control, all the time. As well, it provided no inconsiderable enjoyment and satisfaction—without any hassles of a personal nature! Well, that was apart from those few Claudia was starting to create, she qualified honestly with a sigh. A reminder that not unnaturally prompted thoughts of Dennis, and, feeling appreciably more settled in her mind, she squared her shoulders and made for the phone in order to ring him, as promised.

It took a while to placate him regarding his earlier attempt to talk to her, but the information that she might be able to put in a good word or two on the firm's behalf to no less a person than Talbot Tremayne himself, the head of the whole Tremayne empire, did help considerably to assuage his ruffled feelings.

'Will his son be present at this meeting too?' Dennis went on to enquire enthusiastically.

'Dare?' Teal brows drew together in a frown. 'Well, yes, of course. I'm accompanying . . .'

'No, I meant Reece Tremayne—the other son,' he interrupted to explain a trifle impatiently. 'From what I hear, he's not exactly a nobody within the organisation either.'

'Oh! I didn't know that.' She had met Dare's younger brother on a couple of occasions previously, but only remembered him as a likeable young man attending university. Now it appeared he was assuming the duties the elder Tremayne had always wanted Dare to undertake within the company. 'But as to your question,' she continued, 'since it's a meeting concerning Tremayne Industries, then I imagine he would certainly be there.'

Dennis made a sound of satisfaction, but then seemed to hesitate before hazarding in a more restrained fashion, 'Meanwhile, in view of this meeting tomorrow, I take it you've succeeded in overcoming your reluctance to working with Tremayne on this project?'

Teal swallowed. Little did he know! But of course it was her work here that was all-important to Dennis at the moment. 'That's what you wanted, isn't it?' she parried with a camouflaging half-laugh as a result.

'And on a personal level?'

Her stomach lurched. 'There isn't any *personal* level!' she snapped with more intensity than she intended in her desire to emphasise the point to herself.

'Then I guess Claudia must have got it wrong somehow when she said . . .'

'Yes! Claudia surely was wrong,' she intervened irately. Damn the other girl for being an overly ambitious troublemaker! She really was beginning to use low tactics in her efforts to achieve her own aims! 'Or don't you believe I'm capable of learning from my past mistakes?' She turned the argument back on to Dennis in her annoyance.

'Yes, naturally I do,' he was swift to assure her in a conciliatory tone. 'And I'm sorry. I didn't mean to imply . . .' Breaking off, he expelled a rueful breath. 'I guess I'm just finding it difficult to accept the idea of him escorting you to these places, that's all.'

With her phone call presently and satisfactorily

concluded, Teal collected a clipboard and a pen from her desk and promptly set off for the kiosk. For the moment, at least, she thought it prudent to ensure there was no likelihood of her being alone with Dare again, and noting the requirements Amy would like incorporated within the kiosk's program seemed a good way to kill two birds with one stone. Dare had already outlined the fundamentals he wished the program to include.

None the less, if she had thought the exercise might also have allowed her to expel him from her thoughts through giving her whole attention to the work in hand, she was immediately disabused of the notion on coming face to face with Amy. The girl's expression altered swiftly from cheerfully smiling, as she delivered a tray of refreshments to some visitors seated at one of the tables, to antagonistically glowering as she noted Teal's presence when she returned to the counter.

'What do you want? Come to tell a few more lies, have you?' she sneered in derogatory accents without preamble.

Taken aback, Teal raised her eyebrows in astonishment. 'Lies? What lies?'

'Like the one about you supposedly only being interested in your boss!' Amy hissed.

Teal's breath caught in her throat. Could Dare possibly have said something to the contrary? 'So what makes you think I'm not?' Determinedly, she kept her tone as light as possible.

'Because I watched you after you left the kiosk yesterday. I *saw* the way you were playing up to Dare!

Oh, of course I know about women like you, but . . . it really must have been some green light you were giving him to have had him *kissing* you, even,' Amy's lip curled in scornful disgust, 'within hours of your first meeting!'

Even as she wondered in some discomfort just who else might also have witnessed that particular scene, Teal compelled her features to remain dispassionately schooled. 'Except that yesterday wasn't the first time we'd met,' she revealed on a carefully offhand note. 'As it happens, I was employed by Tremayne Industries many years ago . . . when Dare also used to work for the company.'

It was Amy who looked startled now, her lips parting, although only briefly, and then she clamped them shut again. 'That's still hardly any reason for him to kiss you . . . unless you were blatantly encouraging him!' Her gaze turned smugly disparaging. 'I mean, why else would he bother to pay you any attention . . . at your age?'

On any other occasion Teal would have found it humorous to be evidently considered over the hill at twenty-four, but in view of the circumstances she suspected laughter would neither appease Amy, nor, more important, assist herself. There was one point she did intend to rectify, however.

'Since I can assure you, without qualification, that you're quite wrong in assuming I have any interest whatsoever in any male other than Dennis, my boss, I guess it can only have been purely on the basis of a very old acquaintance,' she said deliberately. 'Until I decided to seek work on the mainland in order to further my career—which, I might add, has always been my prime consideration—Dare and I often had occasion to work quite closely together.' Not all of which was the strict truth, of course, but sufficiently reasonable for Amy's benefit, she considered. Then she added for good measure, 'The reason for it being such a brief kiss . . . as I'm sure you also noticed.' A touch of dulcet sarcasm edged into her voice.

Amy gave a dismissive sniff. 'Then why didn't he say he knew you when he first told us you were coming here?' she demanded, her eyes narrowing suspiciously, and Teal released a long-suffering sigh.

'Most likely because he considered it of too little importance to even rate a mention . . . the same as I do!' she retorted, starting to lose her patience. Didn't she already have enough problems, without having to suffer the interrogation of, according to Dare, an unduly jealous and possessive teenager? 'So now, if you feel you could possibly put your mind to it, do you think we could get on with the work I came to do? After all, just think—the faster I complete it, the quicker I'll be gone from here altogether. A circumstance, I might point out, that will suit me just fine too!' Her tone was not only sharper but openly caustic as well now, and as a result had Amy biting her lip doubtfully.

'Oh—well, I was really only meaning to warn you that you were wasting your time if—if you did have ambitions with regard to Dare,' she put forward in a half deprecatory, half challenging vein. 'I mean, you obviously aren't aware of the depth of our feelings for each other.'

Neither was she, apparently, *if* Dare was to believed, mused Teal. But, since she had no wish to become involved in disputes concerning either claim, she purposely refrained from making any comment that could prove contentious.

In lieu, she merely offered non-committally, 'Yes, well, that's your and Dare's business. Meanwhile, mine is to implement a computer system I'm anxious to have finalised as soon as possible, and towards that end . . .' she eyed the young redhead significantly, 'doubtless Dare would prefer it if it could be accomplished not only smoothly, but swiftly as well. Not least from the point of view of the cost involved in having me here. So shall we make a start with stock control, or is there some other area where you would rather begin?'

Amy lifted a diffident shoulder. 'N-no, stock control sounds OK to me . . . I think,' the last was added with a sickly grimace. And as if she couldn't help herself she followed it on a somewhat wailing note with, 'I'm not sure I even know the sort of information you might want!'

Relieved to at last have the subject of personalities behind them, Teal was able to revert to a more natural manner and smiled reassuringly. 'Of course you do,' she averred. 'To start with, it's simply all the procedures you follow in running the kiosk, that's all.'

'And then?' Amy still didn't look entirely convinced.

'Then once I know those, along with any ideas you may have regarding other capabilities you think could be of assistance to you, I set about designing a program that will enable you to handle it all with far greater ease, certainly more efficiency, *and* in a considerably reduced amount of time.' Pausing, she tilted her head enquiringly, a smile catching at her lips. 'Now the latter, especially, isn't a prospect to cause you any despondency, surely?'

Amy uttered a rueful half-laugh. 'No, I guess not,' she conceded.

With the second half of the day proving far less of a trial than the first, Teal found she could devote herself to her work in an increasingly comfortable frame of mind. Also, in view of the fact that Dare had merely treated her with an easy and agreeable casualness—to her relief, even if tempered with some slight confusion—since that last, and most perturbing incident, her relaxed mood carried over to Thursday, thereby enabling her to view their approaching journey to Hobart and the ensuing meeting in a far more naturally cheerful state.

They left in the middle of the afternoon, planning to arrive in the city around five—this in order to allow time for Dare to drive Teal to her apartment, so she could shower and change, before heading back across the Derwent to the Tremayne home which overlooked Kangaroo Bay on the eastern shore.

Their route took them across the central plateau, past two of the larger and most popular trout-fishing lakes in the craggy and thickly forested highlands, and the sleek Porsche ate up the miles effortlessly. It was a lovely summer's day, the temperature pleasant for travelling, the azure sky only sparsely dotted with light puffs of clouds, and the warm breeze blowing into the car adding to Teal's sense of well-being.

'I suppose your brother joining Tremaynes must have been at least some compensation to your father for your departure from the company,' she hazarded idly as they left the high country behind them and began heading down into the green valley below.

Dare grinned wryly. 'He was certainly grateful we weren't both determined to be independent, that's for sure.' His darkly lashed eyes surveyed her speculatively. 'So who told you Reece was a part of the business now?' There was a momentary pause, his expression taking on a bantering aspect. 'Or have you been making enquiries?'

Teal gave an indolent shake of her head. 'No, Dennis happened to mention it, as a matter of fact.'

'In connection with tonight's meeting, hmm?'

'So? You were the one to suggest I accompany you, after all.'

'And it never occurred to you to wonder why?'

Teal cast him a sidelong glance. 'Well, yes, it occurred to me,' she owned slowly. 'I just didn't care to delve into it too deeply, that's all.' Her lips shaped part ruefully, part mockingly. 'I couldn't be certain I would like the answer.'

Dare laughed, making her heart flutter as his mouth curled engagingly at the corners with amusement. 'Well, well, a completely truthful remark for once,' he drawled. 'Matters would appear to be improving.'

Between them? Teal inhaled shakily at the thought, suddenly aware of the ambivalence of her feelings. On the one hand, she had to admit she found it enjoyable to be able to act more naturally with him, to relax and laugh with him. Hadn't they always shared the same sense of humour? On the other hand, though, she was all too conscious that that could also turn out to hold the most danger for her too.

Heavens above, who knew better than she did just how captivating he could be? If she didn't keep a tight rein on her feelings, she could find herself falling in love with him all over again, and that was something that could never be allowed to happen. No, he could already affect her senses powerfully enough, without arming him with that weapon as well!

Simulating an insouciant stretch, she settled further into her seat. 'It's simply too nice a day for any discord,' she put forward on a light note, and in order to divert his attention to a less hazardous topic continued swiftly, 'On the subject of work, though . . . I've been meaning to ask if you have any preference regarding a particular system, or manufacturer thereof, et cetera.' She turned her head against the red leather to eye him directly. 'Since computers don't all work in the same language, the operating system is crucial from my point of view, and that's quite apart from the fact that you may not even need me to write programs for some functions, because there are standard software packages already available on the market which it would be less expensive to utilise instead.'

Dare spared her an expressive glance. 'I'll take your word for it,' he said drily. 'As for the operating system . . .' he flexed a wide shoulder negligently, 'I leave that wholly to you. That's your field, not mine, so whatever you decide is best, you just purchase what's necessary and I'll take it from there.' He cast her a look filled with lazy raillery. 'I'm in your hands entirely, precious.'

Teal responded with a wry grimace. 'And me with professional ethics to consider,' she grieved mockingly. 'What a lost opportunity!'

'Those are the breaks, I guess.'

With him always remaining untouched, never losing any sleep over his actions? she mused with a sigh. Had it ever been any different where Dare was concerned? Regretting having allowed him to distract her into answering flippantly, she forced an airy shrug.

'Yes, well, we appear to be digressing,' she essayed, and valiantly ignored the brief but disconcertingly astute gaze her defensive reversion attracted. 'There's also the matter of terminals—visual display terminals—to be taken into account, of course. You'll be wanting more than one, I presume?' And, after his confirming nod, 'With networking capabilities?'

Dare's lips twitched. 'Meaning, they each have access to all the information stored?'

Teal couldn't restrain the responding smile that etched its way across her own mouth. 'Put in its simplest terms,' she granted whimsically.

'Then the answer is yes to that too.'

Teal acknowledged his reply with a thoughtful nod. 'It was also mentioned that you could be considering expanding the system to include control of your automation devices as well as just monitoring them,' she relayed, flicking him an enquiring glance. 'Have you had any further thoughts along those lines?'

Dare lifted his shoulders indeterminately. 'You're the expert. Do you think I should?'

'Well, I can see definite advantages in it,' she advised slowly. 'At the same time, however, naturally it would also make the project more costly, and since I don't know the amount you've budgeted for the system, or indeed whether you would consider such advantages worth the outlay, in the final analysis only you can decide if the gains outweigh the additional price involved.'

'Although it would be less expensive to implement it now, along with the rest, rather than have to alter the system at a later date in order to include it?'

Teal nodded. 'Both from the point of view of programming and installation,' she agreed.

'Hmm . . .' Dare assimilated the advice meditatively. 'Then I guess we'd better go over it in detail on Monday—I doubt there'll be time tomorrow—so we can evaluate the pros and cons of the matter.'

For the remainder of the journey their conversation revolved around less specific subjects—light, uncomplicated and humorous ones that left Teal feeling at ease, and even, on occasion, had her breaking up with irrepressible laughter. To give Dare his due, he always had been a vital and appealing companion, she recalled ruefully. It had been one of the things that had first attracted her to him.

Nevertheless, when he eventually brought the Porsche to a halt outside the large old colonial-styled house—gracious, two-storeyed, masses of decorative white cast-iron lacework—where her apartment comprised the whole of the top floor, she experienced an overwhelming reluctance to invite him inside. She found she was averse to having disquieting memories of his unsettling presence forever implanted there.

'You don't have to bother to wait,' she offered quickly with a faltering smile as she opened the door and prepared to alight. 'You'd probably like to shower and change too, and it's no trouble for me to catch a taxi.'

Dare gazed at her askance. 'It's even less trouble for me to wait,' he drawled wryly, pushing open his door, to Teal's dismay. 'And that was my understanding of the arrangement.' Gaining his feet, he began walking round to the passenger side.

With a swallow, Teal scrambled upright herself. 'Although it would save time,' she proposed with pretended helpfulness.

Straightening from locking the car, Dare glanced at the watch encircling his wrist. 'Except that we have plenty of that to spare,' he destroyed her last hope indolently, and, cupping her elbow in his hand, urged her in the direction of the house. 'Upstairs or downstairs?' he questioned as they passed through the white-painted gate.

Teal skimmed the tip of her tongue across her lips and exhaled defeatedly. 'Upstairs,' she revealed in a faint murmur.

Intensely conscious all the while of Dare's hand on her arm, and the nearness of his strongly muscled frame, she was relieved when they at last reached her door and she could put some distance between them on entering the apartment. But, as she noticed him coolly appraising his surroundings, she suddenly seemed to see them with new eyes as well.

From the pale grey upholstered tubular furniture and the smoked-glass and steel bar, to the white, sparsely adorned walls and the careful placement of a number of potted palms, it looked bare, of both charm and warmth . . . and she was stunned. She had always thought of it as tasteful and stylish before, but now, for some unknown reason, she abruptly found herself having second thoughts.

Dare, however, was nowhere near as doubtful. His first glance was sufficient for him to reach, and make known, his verdict.

'Cool, clinical . . . and totally impersonal,' he passed judgement with a certain derision. 'Or was that the whole idea . . . to prevent anyone from guessing that beneath that businesslike exterior there lurks a decidedly more passionate and emotional nature?'

Teal's breathing quickened. 'Which is fortunately tempered with the wisdom of experience now,' she was swift to qualify, deliberately, protectively.

Dare's ensuing smile was openly disbelieving, and in an attempt to defend herself she continued hurriedly, 'In any case, none of that has anything to do with the décor,' she denied. 'Since the high-tech field is often a very social one, most of it was dictated by convenience. Open space and a lack of clutter is far more suitable, as well as advantageous when it comes to cleaning up afterwards, where parties are concerned.'

Dare inclined his head, rather more sardonically than in acceptance, his gold-flecked eyes never leaving her defensively set features. 'Parties which haven't yet resulted in Elford staying the night,' he mused in an infuriatingly chafing drawl. 'How incredibly—disciplined—of him!'

The amusement in his voice rankled. 'Not to mention considerate and estimable!' she shot back in bittersweet accents, her head lifting. 'Now, why don't you make yourself some coffee?' She flung an arm wide to indicate the direction of the kitchen. 'And let me get on with having my shower!' Spinning on her heel, she marched, straight-backed, across the floor and into the largest of the two bedrooms the apartment possessed.

By the time she had finished in the shower and returned to her room to dress, Teal's feelings had subsided markedly. What did it matter to her what Dare thought of the apartment? she dismissed with a shrug as she slipped into a silky, flesh-coloured and lace-trimmed teddy. It suited her and her life-style, that was what was important . . . even if it was a little—she hesitated to put it into words—on the depersonalised side.

Seating herself before her mirror-backed dressing-table, she began brushing her hair rhythmically, soothingly, and then her hand suddenly stilled, her blue eyes widening, as she saw the door opening behind her and Dare calmly entering with a pottery mug in his hand.

'I thought you might like a coffee as well,' he said casually, resting a hand on her shoulder and leaning forward to deposit the mug on the dressing-table.

A quiver of unadulterated awareness curled through

Teal's insides, riveting her to her seat as she stared at him, transfixed, in the mirror. He acted as if the past five years had never happened, as if they—lived together! she thought bemusedly. While she . . . She felt unnerved by his mere presence, let alone his lazily presumptuous gaze; she felt insecure, half naked. She *was* half naked, came the almost hysterical amendment that did little to lessen either her self-consciousness or her inner ferment.

'I—well . . . y-you might at least have knocked,' she just managed to stammer, finding her voice at last.

Dare laughed—a soft, throaty sound that made her heart race, and seemed to graze every sensitive area of her suddenly overly receptive body. 'I do know what you look like without clothes, my pet,' he drawled. 'We've even been known to share a bed, remember?' He traced a burning path down her exposed spine with a forefinger, and she couldn't deny the mad leaping of her pulse, even as she shook her head in repudiation.

'Th-that was a long time ago, and—and has nothing to do with the present,' she claimed unsteadily.

'Doesn't it?' Dare moved a step closer, and she could feel the disturbing warmth of him against her back, could draw in the fresh, vibrant male smell of him. 'Who are you trying to persuade—me . . . or yourself?'

'You, naturally!' Her voice had a thin, strangled sound to it. 'I d-don't need any persuading to know I did the right thing in ending our—our relationship.'

Dare stroked the soft skin of her shoulders, jolting her with the strength of feeling—of shockingly

physical desire, damn it!—that splintered through her.
'Even though you're still no more indifferent to me
than I am to you?' he countered on a roughly
thickening note, sliding his hands down to cup her
breasts possessively, and Teal was immobilised with
horror by the way in which they immediately swelled
at his touch, the nipples hardening and thrusting
betrayingly against his palms. Dare uttered a sound of
triumphant satisfaction. 'At least your body's more
truthful than you are!'

Now Teal succeeded in moving, whirling to her feet
agitatedly, her curving form suffused with heat. 'All
right, I admit that—that whatever was between us
isn't—isn't entirely dead,' she conceded painfully,
trembling. 'But—but that still doesn't mean I'm
interested in resuming any—any physical liaison.'

'No?' He regarded her with darkened eyes as he
started towards her, making her back away nervously
until halted by the dressing-table.

Oh, where was the crisp and poised career woman
now? she despaired. He was reducing her to an
unassured adolescent again!

'No,' she said, but in a huskily shaky tone that
dismayingly sounded less than categorical even to her
own ears.

A slow, seductive smile shaped Dare's mouth, warm
with a masculine knowledge that turned her lips dry.
'You don't even say the word with conviction,' he
murmured with gentle mockery, his hand finding her
nape and beginning to caress the susceptive skin.

Teal's breathing became ragged, and she
instinctively put her hands against his chest in an

effort to provide some sort of barrier, however slight, between them. 'Th-that's still not to imply . . .'

'That you don't mean it?' Tilting her face up to his, he brushed his lips across hers tantalisingly, lingering at the corners, teasing them with his tongue. 'Then don't you think it's about time you changed your mind?' he muttered throatily against her unconsciously parted mouth, and, as if unable to help himself, he reclaimed her lips with a hungry, demanding urgency.

Think about changing her mind? Teal couldn't think at all. Not now, while he was holding her so close, while his mouth and tongue tasted her, while memories of their previous lovemaking assailed her so treacherously. She could only feel, and surrender helplessly to the engulfing emotions he was so skilfully stimulating.

Her hands were still trapped between them, but with no thought of resistance now. Instead, they slipped around him to explore and savour again the ridged muscularity of his broad back, and with a shuddering intake of breath Dare caught her up in his arms and swiftly carried her across to the bed.

In the back of Teal's mind the thought dimly surfaced that it was madness for her not to stop him, but, when she felt his hard and virile length next to her, her arms gave the lie to any such warning as they clasped him tightly to her. Linking about his neck, her hands pulled his head down until their mouths met once more in a heated, devouring kiss that erased every thought from her mind except for the intoxicating feel and taste of him.

It seemed her whole body ached for him, for his touch, and when he slid her flimsy covering down to her hips and his caressing hands found the throbbing fullness of her bared breasts a husky moan of undeniable satisfaction escaped her. Breathless with the intensity of her emotions, she quivered as his fingers explored the swelling curves, brushed back and forth across the sensitive nipples until they were taut with need, and then gasped deep in her throat at the white-hot pleasure that consumed her when finally he drew one of those erect and eager crests between his lips.

Moist and insistent, the hungry pull of his mouth inflamed her every erotic nerve-ending so that she strained against him with an urgency she had no control over, her blood on fire, her body frantic with longing. Oh, lord, he was making her want him as much as she ever had, Teal recognised dazedly. But in that mad, rapturous instant she didn't much care. Hadn't he always possessed an attraction, an animal magnetism, that had drawn her to him like a positive charge of electricity to a negative one? she was honest enough with herself to admit.

When Dare finally released her swollen nipple, Teal was filled with a feeling of dismay, not wanting the stirring pleasure to stop. Then, realising it was only in order that he might claim its counterpart, she knew a sense of relief and, with her fingers digging deeply into his hair, gave herself up once more to the fiery arousal of his rhythmically drawing mouth as it tugged and suckled greedily at her aching breast.

They both registered the sound of the front door

opening at exactly the same time. Dare reluctantly raised his head to a listening position, the rest of his body tensing, ready for instant action, even as his eyes delved questioningly into Teal's startled though still partly bemused ones.

'Elford?' In spite of his low tone, there was a harsh rasp in the query that made her blink.

'No!' she denied in a muted but indignant murmur. 'No one has a key other than myself, and——' She came to a sudden halt with her eyes widening, and glistening white teeth catching at her lower lip. 'Oh, lord, I gave one to Mrs Birrell, my landlady who lives in the apartment below, so she could come in to water my plants while I was away.' The revelation was made with an anguished groan.

'You're sure that's who it is?'

As if to confirm it, the sound of a container being filled with water came from the kitchen and Teal nodded half ruefully, half thankfully, before pushing herself up against the pillows and beginning to rearrange her scanty underwear.

Relaxed again, Dare rolled on to his side, and caught hold of her wrist to prevent her from sliding the second of the straps on to her shoulder. 'I preferred you the way you were,' he said softly, relinquishing his grip in order to cover her bare breast with his hand.

Teal trembled violently, suspecting she preferred it that way too. 'But—but Mrs Birrell . . .' she protested breathlessly, struggling for reason against her own wayward inclinations as her surging nipple pressed against his warm flesh.

Dare shrugged, and bent to caress the silky skin of her shoulder sensuously with his mouth. 'Since she evidently doesn't realise you're here, why not just close the bedroom door, and . . .' His words trailed away implicitly as he swept his hand down to her hip and along her thigh.

Teal's breath caught in her throat, but although she couldn't deny the strong attraction of his suggestion she shook her head wildly in negation. 'We can't!' she just succeeded in gasping, frantic at both the thought of succumbing and of discovery in such an intimate situation. 'I—I have to let her know I'm here! Otherwise she might hear us, and—and guess what's happening, when she waters those.' She flung out an arm to indicate through the lace curtains the plant-filled tubs on the balcony just outside the bedroom.

'And would that be so terribly shocking if she did guess?' he hazarded drily.

'To Mrs Birrell . . . yes!' she affirmed emphatically, although continuing to keep her voice low. 'You don't understand. She's nearly eighty, and her ideas on morality were formed in the first half of this century when social conventions were far more strict, and *ladies*, as she's wont to remark, did not indulge in permissive behaviour.'

Dare's mouth sloped crookedly. 'Meaning, you're worried she might want to cancel your lease if she found out?'

Teal shook her head. 'I doubt she would. She's not that type of person.' She uttered a helpless sigh. 'She's just a sweet little old lady who's been very kind to me, and whom I wouldn't like to . . . well, shock or disappoint, I suppose.'

Moving slightly, Dare set his lips to the curve where her neck met her shoulder and stroked upwards with his tongue. 'Although you've no such aversion to disappointing me,' he chided huskily, his breath warm against her ear, and Teal swallowed convulsively.

'Dare . . . please!' she turned her head to entreat, one hand lifting to press restrainingly against his shoulder. 'If I don't get out there soon . . .' She scrambled to slide her legs over the side of the bed.

'OK, OK, I know defeat when it's staring me in the face. You're free to go,' he allowed with a smile twitching at his shapely mouth. But, as she prepared to rise to her feet, his arms wrapped around her, drawing her back against his strong chest. 'Provided you grant me a raincheck,' he added in a teasing whisper beside her ear.

Teal's stomach constricted. 'Dare!' she remonstrated on a strangled note, glowering at him over her shoulder.

'You can't blame a man for trying,' he drawled impenitently, his smile widening and his arms loosening.

'Oh!' Springing to her feet, Teal spun vexedly to face him, but the sight of his disarmingly laughing expression proved too much to overcome, and her own mouth began to pull into a responding grin. 'You're . . . you're incorrigible!' she denounced helplessly before hurrying to pull on a wrap and leave the room in order to tell Mrs Birrell that it wouldn't be necessary for her to water the plants that afternoon.

CHAPTER SIX

THE EVENING was a very enjoyable one for Teal.

With Mrs Birrell's departure had come a return of prudence, assisted by the fact that now, of necessity, she had to do the watering herself—an excuse she used blatantly to keep Dare at a distance. Dear heaven, even after all these years, it seemed he still only had to touch her, kiss her, lean that so very vitally male body against hers, and she lost whatever willpower or strength of purpose she possessed!

The Tremayne family, who included Reece's new wife, were as charmingly agreeable as she remembered; their expressed pleasure at seeing her again obviously genuine. And dinner—a delicious mixture of hot and cold dishes, the accompanying wines smooth and heady to the taste—was a pleasantly extended affair as the conversation flowed freely around the magnificent carved oak table.

The subjects were many and varied—amusing, serious, inconsequential—although not unexpectedly, since that was the reason for the gathering, Tremayne business occupied a large portion of their attention. However, far from the discussion being ponderous, Teal discovered herself becoming more and more interested as the time passed, and especially when it became apparent that the thoughts and opinions of the women at the table, including herself, were not only welcome, but actively sought.

It was also something of an eye-opener in other ways as well, she found—not least, regarding Dare. For, where once she had considered him foolishly indifferent, frivolous even, in his attitude towards both work and his family's business interests, now she gradually began to realise he really was just too much of an individualist to have ever fitted into such a predetermined mould. Or perhaps she was able to recognise it now because of the changes experience had wrought in herself, she speculated. Regardless of the cause, it was more than evident to her now that Dare could only ever be his own man, accepting the challenge of making and mastering his own destiny.

He was the one in the family with the skill and flair of the entrepreneur—Reece possessing the cautionary steadiness and analytical mind of the accountant; their father having the ability to visualise the total concept, and the drive to put it into practice and make it work. Together, they made a formidable combination, and noticing the way in which the whole family fed off the others' ideas Teal had no doubt they could only continue to prosper further in the years to come.

When they finally retired after dinner to the veranda that overlooked the still waters of the moon-silvered river to the myriad lights of the city on the far shore, amid the debate concerning the mooted proposal for another Tremayne Industries takeover, it was Dare who gradually brought the conversation around to the side issue of computer systems and consultants—much to Teal's surprise. Although he had said the occasion would be a good opportunity for her to put in a word or two for ICS, she certainly hadn't anticipated any assistance from him in introducing the subject.

'Of course, with those systems being Teal's sphere of activity, there wouldn't be any personal prejudice on your part regarding the relative merits thereof,' Reece immediately commented on a dry note, eyeing his brother banteringly.

Dare merely grinned and favoured Teal with a lazily indulgent wink that turned her heart upside-down. 'Naturally there is,' he both astonished her and made her feel somewhat self-conscious by averring. Both his and Reece's remark seemed to imply that she and Dare were a twosome again, and in spite of the events of the afternoon her mind at least was still defiant at the thought. 'None the less, and as you should know,' his gaze was wry as it held his brother's, 'when business is involved, it's facts, not associations—of any kind—that dictate my actions.'

Reece gave a ruefully acknowledging nod, leaving it to their father to mourn, though not without some evident pride, 'Even to the extent of refusing any kind of connection with Tremayne Industries. With the plans I know you have in mind, I sometimes get the feeling your ultimate aim is to take *us* over!'

'Uh-uh!' Dare denied with a laugh, shaking his head. 'I'm afraid my feelings concerning paper manufacture, printing, industrial engineering and so forth are still the same as they always were. Whereas with regard to aquaculture, in all its varying forms, and with fishing fleet catches decreasing all round the world . . . well, that's something else again. The possibilities are almost limitless, and particularly in this country where the climate ranges from the wet tropics right through to the alpine.'

'With all ventures computer-controlled?' put in Reece seriously.

Dare executed an indeterminate shrug. 'At the moment, for the trout farm at least, *controlled* still remains to be discussed . . . but definitely computer-monitored. The benefits provided are just too numerous to ignore.'

His brother nodded and, with his thoughts returned to a matter that obviously came within his area of influence at Tremaynes, spent the next half-hour or so in discussion with Teal regarding various aspects of her work, as well as that of Integrated Computer Systems.

'Thank you for introducing the subject of systems analysis and programming,' Teal turned to the man beside her to acknowledge with a warm smile as they headed down the drive some time later. 'Reece—and your father too—seemed quite interested in some of the projects ICS have undertaken. I know Dennis will be pleased when I tell him.'

Dare's lips twisted expressively. 'To hell with Dennis,' he responded in a wry drawl. Coming to the roadway, he brought the car to a halt, his hand lifting to cup her chin. 'I did it for you, not him.'

In the dim interior of the vehicle, his amber eyes appeared to reflect a light that was even more untamed than usual, and Teal's lips parted in an unconsciously provocative fashion. 'Then I appreciate your efforts on my behalf, and you can take satisfaction in knowing that I'm very pleased as well,' she returned huskily. She hesitated, her expression curious. 'Although I must admit I'm not sure just why you should have done me, and therefore ICS, such a favour.'

Dare shrugged and, releasing her, turned the Porsche on to the road. 'It was what you wanted, wasn't it?'

Well, more correctly, what Dennis desired, Teal amended silently. Aloud, she put forward, with increasing awkwardness, 'Even so, there was still—no reason for you to have made it possible after—after what happened all those years ago.'

'Not even out of the sheer goodness of my heart?' he quipped.

Her mouth tilted ruefully. 'Except that only minutes before initially suggesting it, you were being unbearably disparaging.'

'Me?' The glance he flicked her was filled with humorous mock-disbelief.

'Yes, you!' she retorted with a helpless smile.

'And now?' A captivating curve swept across his mouth with all the heart-stopping appeal she remembered so well, making her feel suddenly breathless as a rush of ungovernable feeling, of yearning, abruptly assaulted her senses.

Teal's mind reeled, and if she hadn't already been seated she knew her legs would have given way beneath her. She'd had no need to worry that she might fall in love with Dare again, because she had never damn well fallen *out* of love with him! The sudden realisation forced its way into her shocked and dismayed consciousness. Notwithstanding all her efforts and assurances to herself to the contrary, it was all too glaringly obvious that she hadn't ever forgotten him, let alone succeeded in expelling him from her heart. She was as much in love with him now as she had ever been! He had provoked, mocked and enticed her until she couldn't think straight and her emotions were beyond her control. For all her struggles and protestations, her heart was back in his keeping—vulnerably, waywardly—and there didn't seem to be a solitary thing she could do about it!

Moreover, he was still awaiting a reply to his last question and, swallowing heavily, she schooled her features carefully before venturing to finally respond as they joined the freeway leading to the Tasman bridge and the city.

'Now . . . I think you'd better concentrate on your driving,' she evaded a touch throatily, but still in as insouciantly droll a vein as she could engineer. A passing car cutting in recklessly close in front of them fortuitously added substance to her suggestion, making Dare nod graphically in agreement as he smoothly took evasive action.

The rest of the journey was accomplished without any further complications, and a short time later the Porsche was pulling to a halt outside the garden and shrub-surrounded building containing Teal's apartment.

'I'll see you to your door,' Dare said, removing his keys from the ignition and already starting to open the door, but Teal shook her head quickly in protest.

'There's really no need,' she pushed out, her pulse thudding apprehensively in her throat. She was uncertain as to his intentions and, with the devastating revelation concerning her own feelings so fresh in her mind, even less sure of what she wanted. 'There's no likelihood of anyone attacking me,' she added with faint humour as her fingers sought the door-handle.

'Although you did believe you might have had a prowler in the apartment this afternoon,' he reminded her pointedly before alighting and calmly walking around the car to open her door.

'Mistakenly,' she was swift to qualify as he assisted her to her feet, and his mouth crooked obliquely.

'Stop being so obstructive! I said I would take you *home* . . . and that's up there.' He indicated the top floor, and with a hand in the small of her back began directing her towards the front door.

Once inside, Teal led the way nervously upstairs, but made no move to actually enter the apartment after unlocking the door and turning the light on in order to prove, albeit by a somewhat facetious gesture, that it was free of any intruder.

However, instead of making any move towards the room, or even suggesting they should do so, Dare took her completely by surprise by merely remarking, 'I guess I'll see you in the morning, then. I'll pick you up around nine, all right?'

Teal nodded mechanically, a sudden and utterly ridiculous feeling of perfidious disappointment besetting her. 'You—you're not coming in?' she had faltered before even realising what she was saying.

Dare tensed, his thickly lashed eyes locking unwaveringly with hers. 'Are you inviting me?' His voice was deep and low.

She circled her lips with her tongue, her breathing shallow. 'Do you want—an invitation?' The question seemed to come of its own volition.

He caught her head between his hands, his fingers threading within the honey-coloured strands of her hair, uncustomary lines of strain marking the taut set of his shapely mouth. 'You already know the answer to that,' he growled on a roughened note. 'More than ever, I want . . . you!' He fastened his mouth to hers with a searing, devastating intensity she couldn't resist.

Melting against him, Teal wrapped her arms tightly about him, her lips willingly parting beneath the probing pressure of his tongue as wild tides of desire flooded through her, flowing like molten fire. She loved him, wanted him, wanted him inside her, she acknowledged shakily, and her limbs turned languid at the thought.

'Heaven help me . . . *how* I want you!' Dare groaned thickly at length, and she realised in surprise that he wasn't entirely in control of his emotions either.

'I—I thought you meant to leave,' she breathed unevenly, chewing at her lip, and his arms wrapped about her convulsively.

'Only because of your concern for your landlady's sensibilities,' he disclosed with a husky wryness. There was a slight pause. 'Although, since she does appear to have retired for the night . . .' There had been no lights at all shining from any of the windows downstairs. 'Do you want me to go?' His tone deepened as he regarded her tautly with eyes that were dark with feeling.

Teal trembled. She knew she should reply in the affirmative, but how could she, feeling about him the way she did? She could no more control the love she felt for him than she could the rapid beat of her pulse. And right now that love was filling her with a craving to feel his hard and urgent body pressed close to hers again, and to experience the consuming fulfilment of his intimate possession.

'I . . . oh, no,' she owned on a fervently sighed breath, her fingers entangling within his dark hair at the back of his head, and with a muffled groan his mouth captured hers once more, at the same time as he scooped her into his arms and strode into the apartment.

Closing the door behind them with his foot, he carried her through to the bedroom, only then breaking the hungry contact of his lips on hers when he laid her gently on the bed. Leaning over her, he caressed the delicate contours of her face with his hand, his fingers lingering against her mouth until, as if starved of its sweetness, he claimed it again in a compelling, plundering kiss that stole her breath and made her quiver with the force of her own needs and passions.

Almost fiercely, his tongue filled and explored the moist warmth of her mouth, stirring them both as her lips opened wider to allow him to savour her more deeply, her own tongue flirting and entwining with his in return.

Swiftly, Dare moved to dispose of the frustrating restriction of their clothing, and, as anxious as he for the feel of firm, bronzed muscles pressed to silken, pliant skin, Teal eagerly facilitated their removal. His flesh was warm and smooth beneath her fingertips, and she revelled in being able to explore the sinewed length of his superbly conditioned body at will. Dear heaven, how could she ever have persuaded herself he meant nothing to her any more? she wondered dazedly. He needed only to kiss her, to caress her, and she was vibrantly aware of every sense she possessed. Senses that centred on him, on her need and want of him, and seemingly bound her to him as inextricably as if by inescapable means.

Ripples of ecstasy radiated through her, along with a throbbing ache that was growing in intensity. His mouth was like fire against her sensitive flesh, igniting a matching flame within, and stunning her with the strength of her emotions. Overwhelming desires only Dare had ever been capable of kindling, and satisfying.

Now the fire within turned to a raging inferno that encompassed her entire being, and Teal writhed against him frenziedly, her neck arching, her hands clamping tightly to his dark head, wanting him to cease the exquisite torture, wanting him to continue, wanting . . .

And at last Dare answered her body's demand. With a low groan, he slid his long body upwards, covering her, and she lifted her hips to meet him as with one smooth stroke he embedded himself within her silken, receptive warmth. Feeling herself stretch to accommodate the aching fullness of him, Teal uttered a husky moan of fulfilment, the hard heat of him sheathed so deeply inside her filling her with a rapturous delight, her senses oblivious to everything but him.

Clutching at his shoulders, she pulled his head down to hers, their mouths meeting in an impassioned fusion that stifled her cries of pleasure as he began to move insistently within her. Surging ever deeper with each quickening thrust which she responded to with fierce abandon, he filled her again and again until they were both breathing raggedly. To experience such a consuming sensation once more, to have him inside her so that they were as one, indivisible, was almost more than she could bear.

Her body strained towards his, her legs tightening convulsively about him, and then suddenly tremors of explosive feeling were shaking her whole body as release finally came in a soaring ascent of the senses, and, driving to the liquid depths of her, Dare shuddered his pleasure against her quivering length.

Quietly, they continued to lie together for some time as the tempo of their breathing slowed, Dare not immediately withdrawing from her, but remaining buried within her savouring body. Their skin glistened with a fine sheen of perspiration and, smoothing her tousled hair back from a dampened temple, he bent to kiss her lingeringly.

'No matter how you may like to deny it, I say we belong together,' he muttered hoarsely.

Basking in the warmth of his continuing possession, Teal made a helpless movement. Having welcomed his lovemaking so unreservedly, and feeling as languid and sated as she did in the aftermath, how could she dispute the claim? In spite of everything she loved him, and, although her head might call her heart foolish for wanting him back in her life, want him she did, and no more would she lie to herself about it. No other man had ever stirred her deepest emotions as he did, and deep down she knew no other man could ever make her feel like this again either. When she was in his arms, his hard and powerful body surrounding her, it seemed that nothing else mattered but that they were together.

With an expressive sigh, she entwined slender arms about his neck, an indolent curve beginning to catch at her mouth. 'You thought my actions . . . a denial?' she ventured to tease, eyeing their position significantly.

For a moment their gazes held, and the expression in his—dark, caressing—took her breath away. 'I thought your actions . . . glorious,' he amended on a deep note, and took her mouth lightly, nibbling at her lower lip, drawing it between his own. 'As are you.'

Teal's pulse accelerated. 'I must admit you appear to hold a certain—slight—attraction yourself,' she breathed against his sensuous mouth.

Dare drew back a space, his eyes narrowing, the audacious gleam suddenly appearing within them sending a tingle of excitement coursing through her veins. 'Slight?' he challenged softly, his lips scorching a path to her breasts to tantalise and arouse.

'Well, maybe not slight, exactly,' she just managed to gasp.

His hands took the place of his mouth. 'What then . . .?' he glanced up to ask with a look that made her melt inside.

She shook her head, smiling softly and delighting in every touch of his stroking fingers. 'You're not making it easy.'

'I wasn't intending to,' he murmured in whimsical tones, and ran a hand down the length of her curving body.

Teal's arms tightened, drawing him closer. 'Then you'll be pleased to know you're succeeding.'

'Oh, I'm very pleased about that, you can be sure,' Dare replied huskily, and she sucked in a pleasurable, quivering breath on feeling him beginning to harden and grow inside her as his mouth captured hers possessively . . .

'Dare . . .?' Drowsily, Teal put out a searching hand towards the other side of the bed. Something had disturbed her contented slumber. Probably the fact that his strongly protective body was no longer moulded so comfortingly close to hers, she surmised with lethargic ruefulness, until, as she discovered his presence to be absent altogether, every vestige of languor promptly departed and her eyes flew open in surprise. The room was still shadowed, dawn only just starting to break, but enabling her to just make out his tall figure all the same as he donned his clothes that had been so haphazardly discarded the night before. 'You're leaving?' she quizzed, pushing herself up on one elbow, and the throaty sound of disappointment in her tone had her cheeks colouring.

Turning quickly at the sound of her voice, Dare moved in the direction of the bed. 'Regrettably,' he confirmed with a crooked smile, seating himself on the edge of the mattress. Then, brushing his knuckles against her cheek, 'I'm sorry. Did I wake you?'

Teal dismissed his apology with a shake of her head. 'But if you—really don't want to leave, then . . . why?' Her gaze sought his self-consciously, and a touch apprehensively, in the darkness.

'Only because circumstances seem to dictate it, believe me,' came the gruff assurance. 'I have my gear to collect from home, not to mention requiring the means of shaving which I doubt you can supply, and . . .' his lips twitched wryly, 'there continues to be the matter of your landlady. The car's still outside, and I thought you would prefer it if that wasn't the case when she got up, and then saw us leave together in it some hours later.' He stroked a finger across her lower lip. 'That would be something of a giveaway, don't you think?'

'I guess so,' she had little option but to accede, regretfully, and impulsively she turned her lips against the palm that lingered by her cheek.

Dare's response was immediate. His hand slid to the

back of her head, the better to urge her lips up to his. 'Although if you keep doing things like that, I'm likely not to give a damn about Mrs Birrell,' he promised on a thickening note, and set his mouth to hers with a compelling hunger that had her heart pounding raggedly. Releasing her at last, he set her away from him determinedly, if with evident reluctance, his lips shaping obliquely. 'So go back to sleep, precious, and let me leave while I'm still of a mind to. I'll be back about nine, OK?' He lazily ruffled her already rumpled hair, and rose lithely to his feet.

Smiling, Teal nodded, but when she sank back on to the pillows after his departure her expression gradually assumed a more sober cast as, without his distracting presence, the full significance of her reckless behaviour slowly and disquietingly made itself felt.

So she had discovered she still loved him, and wanted him, *desperately* even! she mocked brutally. But what of today, tomorrow, and all the tomorrows to come? No matter how intoxicating or satisfying his lovemaking might be, was she prepared to accept that as sufficient, knowing his actions were governed by a desire that had nothing to do with love? Dimly, dismayingly, she suspected she might have been, for a while at least, and hastily buried the thought deep in the recesses of her mind.

Besides, hadn't she already warned herself about taking Dare seriously, about him perhaps exacting revenge? After all, he would surely consider it sweetly poetic if he succeeded in having an affair with her—for the second time! And then only until he felt the need for variety, *again*, of course, she reminded herself bitterly, inwardly despairing over the painful and humiliating memories the recollection evoked.

Furthermore, what about Dennis? the sudden thought intruded, and had her chewing guiltily at her lip as a result. So much for her arbitrary contention that *she* didn't practise two-timing! Shame washed over her hotly as she remembered just how unconscionably she had forgotten the other man.

Hadn't it only been two days ago that she had challenged him over his apparent belief that she was incapable of learning from past mistakes? Perturbingly, it appeared she wasn't, and she twisted restively against the pillows, any thought of further sleep completely out of the question now as she struggled to subdue the wayward yearnings of her heart with the controlled prudence of her mind.

CHAPTER SEVEN

On Dare's return to her apartment, Teal was waiting for him on the porch, but when he bent to brush his lips lightly against hers she turned her head aside quickly so that his disturbing mouth connected with her cheek only.

Momentarily, he drew back slightly as he gazed at her askance, then, executing a negligent hunch of a muscular denim-covered shoulder, he relieved her of her overnight bag and turned for the path. 'Mrs Birrell doesn't approve of kissing, either?' he quizzed wryly, espying that woman picking some flowers at the far end of the garden.

Teal moistened her lips. 'She—er—it may have embarrassed her,' she faltered evasively, and, with a wave to the woman in question, hurried ahead of him towards the car.

Having seen her seated and her bag deposited on the back seat, Dare was soon sliding his long length in beside her. 'She can't see us from here,' he promptly proposed, indicating the densely leaved shrubs lining the fence, which did indeed block them from view. 'And you look just too desirable this morning to ignore . . . even if I wanted to.' A hand was suddenly cradling her head, impelling her nearer, and before she could evade it his mouth took possession of hers with all the skill and sensuous allure she both loved and feared.

Deeply thankful for the gear console that prevented him drawing her even closer, Teal held herself stiffly, trying to remain unaffected. Although when his tongue circled her lips, seeking entry, she was shocked and shaken by the treacherous rush of insidious excitement that enveloped her, and she snatched herself free in breathless desperation.

'Yes—well, I think it—it's time we were going,' she pushed out jerkily, keeping her eyes averted. And, casting about frantically for a diversion, 'The—er—weather looks as if it's about to break, and it could be a long trip if a fog closes in on the highlands.' In truth, the cloud cover had been increasing all morning, until now the sky was completely blanketed in darkening grey.

'Hmm . . .' She was unnervingly aware of Dare contemplating her profile speculatively for a few moments before finally turning his gaze skywards. 'You could be right,' he granted in somewhat rueful accents at length. 'Storms were forecast for today, as it happens.'

'Shall we go, then?' Teal's voice immediately became more enthusiastic at the prospect, and his mouth shaped crookedly in response.

'You're very anxious,' he mocked. 'I wasn't aware you were nervous of storms.'

She flushed and shook her head. 'I'm not,' she declared with feigned calm. 'I simply prefer not to drive in fog if it's avoidable, that's all.'

Briefly, Dare looked sceptical, then shrugged and bent forward to start the engine. 'In that case, I guess perhaps we'd better make tracks,' he said offhandedly, and disconcertingly Teal couldn't decide whether she felt relieved or dejected by the indifference in his tone.

To keep her mind from dwelling on it, she concentrated on the scenery as they left Hobart, heading north through the green and peaceful rural areas of the Midlands and the beautiful Clyde Valley; the old stone buildings of the villages they passed through bringing a colonial atmosphere to the scene.

Today, however, the valleys exuded a feeling of waiting almost as they lay dim and quiet beneath the ever-darkening clouds that were rolling in from the west with increasing speed, driven by a fitful wind that came in such mounting gusts that eventually it was to the weather that Teal gave her undivided attention.

'Well, at least with this wind blowing there shouldn't be any fog when we reach the top,' she remarked in a wryly musing voice as they began their ascent to the central plateau.

'No,' Dare was prepared to accede, in equally expressive tones. 'Although if it becomes much stronger, it could be flying branches and the like slowing our progress instead.'

Teal's expression turned rueful. She hadn't thought of that. 'Perhaps it will die down a little once it finally starts to rain,' she proposed hopefully.

'Perhaps,' came the laconic endorsement, but in such a way that, rather than encouraging her, it gave her cause to eye him a trifle dubiously.

'You don't think it will?'

Dare shrugged imperceptibly. 'Let's just say I have my doubts.' His eyes glanced upwards briefly. 'I only know that's one hell of a storm building up there.'

Teal sighed and nodded. It was certainly that, she had to concede, and merely hoped that, since it had managed to hold off so far, it might continue to do so until they reached the farm.

Unfortunately, it didn't. They were only half-way across the plateau when the sky was abruptly streaked by a blinding flash of lightning, followed by an almost ear-splitting crack of thunder, and the heavens opened with a torrent of rain that lashed relentlessly at the vehicle. With it, the wind rose in intensity, whipping up the waters of the lakes so they resembled the sea, and buffeting the swaying trees so violently that it seemed impossible they could continue to withstand its battering force. Not surprisingly, some of them couldn't, as first leaves and twigs and then whole boughs began to give way under the fierce onslaught, to be hurled haphazardly through the air before crashing to the ground.

Nor did it make driving any easier, either, as gusts of wind caught the car and determinedly attempted to force it off course. It simply added to the tension and hazards of the appalling conditions as the rain limited their visibility to a few yards, and the flying debris contributed its own perils.

'Should we stop?' Teal asked worriedly at one point, raising her voice to overcome the pounding of the rain on the roof, but Dare shook his head, his hands taut about the wheel in his efforts to prevent control of the car being wrested from him.

'Without any cover, there's no guarantee we wouldn't be hit by something, anyway. Not least, a falling tree.' They had already seen a few down; one nearly blocking the whole roadway. He flashed her a bantering smile, his teeth gleaming whitely in the unnaturally dim light. 'But don't worry, we'll make it. I'm not about to let you come to any harm.'

Except from the damage he inflicted himself, Teal qualified shakily to herself, and resolutely returned her attention to the wet and shining black ribbon of road in front of them. It was so dark now that it was almost like night. The only illumination, apart from their headlights, coming from the brilliant flashes of jagged lightning that continued to rend the sky.

Teal had hoped that when at last they began their descent from the highlands the storm might not be quite so savage at the lower altitudes, but she was disappointed. As they slowly, carefully, made their way down to the foothills, it soon became apparent that nowhere was to escape its fury. Now they had earthslides to contend with as well and, just as a last straw, with only another two miles to go before reaching the farm, a tree lying diagonally across the road from one side to the other.

'Oh, no!' was Teal's immediate and ruefully grimaced response. Then, sitting forward, she glanced sidelong at Dare, her eyes beginning to shine. 'Or do you think we might just manage to push it far enough to one side to squeeze past it?' They obviously couldn't drive round it as it was. The trunk was too close to the sloping hillside at one end, while the top branches reached to the cliff's edge at the other.

'It's a possibility that occurred to me,' Dare allowed with an answering smile. 'Fortunately, it's not as large as some. Wait here, and I'll give it a go.' He was out of the car within seconds, and running towards the tree as fast as the wind would allow.

Mere moments later, with her eyes half closed against the stinging rain and her clothes feeling as if they were being torn from her, Teal was following him.

'What in hell . . .!' Dare burst out on seeing her appear beside him. He shook his head. 'You should have stayed in the car. There was no need for you to get soaked as well!' he shouted above the wind.

Teal grinned unconcernedly. 'I beg to differ!' she yelled back. 'Apart from the fact that I would have felt guilty being all nice and dry while you tackled it on your own, there is such a thing as many hands making light work, you know. I may not be Wonder Woman, but I can at least help make it a little easier for you.'

Dare laughed and planted a swift kiss on her wet lips. 'OK, partner, you push and I'll pull,' he drawled, before agilely vaulting the tree trunk and taking hold of a solid branch on the other side.

Taking up her own position, Teal kept her head bent. The feel of his mouth against hers was lingering far longer than she wanted, and the knowledge vexed and disturbed her. Damn! Why couldn't she just ignore him? was her last despairing thought before the concerted effort of all her senses was required elsewhere.

Luckily, the downward incline of the road was in their favour, but even so it still took them some considerable time, and many muscle-straining attempts, to move the tree gradually a sufficient distance to provide a large enough gap for the car to scrape through. Although the tree wasn't fully grown—mercifully—it was heavy with water, and the wind hadn't helped at all in the way it had kept blowing the leaves and outer sprigs into their faces.

But at last, drenched to the skin and sprinkled with those persistently clinging wet leaves, they were able to return to the car, and Teal sank gratefully into her seat.

'Lord, I feel like something that's been washed up on the beach!' she exclaimed with a rueful half-laugh, combing her fingers through her dripping and wildly dishevelled hair.

As he surveyed her leisurely, Dare's smiling expression gradually assumed a more enigmatic aspect. 'Nevertheless, quite the most appealing piece of jetsam I've ever seen,' he returned on a deepening note, and, looking down, Teal realised that her T-shirt was soaked just about to transparency.

Self-consciously, she dragged at the clinging fabric, trying to stop it sticking, but each time without success. The moment she let go, it immediately cleaved to her just as revealingly again, the friction of the agitated movements making her sensitive nipples throb, and to her mortification seeming to protrude even more noticeably.

'Yes—well . . .' She broke off helplessly, shaking her head. 'You still don't have to keep looking at me like that!' she rounded on him in vexation.

'Like what?' Dare's gaze was dark and disturbingly warm as he moved fractionally closer, and Teal was nervously aware of the arm that he rested along her seat, his fingers toying absently with her wet hair. 'As if I want to hold you . . . touch you?' He sucked in an audible breath. 'How could I not?' he countered heavily, pulling her nearer, and his mouth found her parted lips.

No! her mind promptly rejected in panic, but alarmingly her body paid no heed to any such attempted defiance as it once again took control, and proceeded to respond to his searing touch with an increasing fervour she couldn't prevent.

Teal couldn't believe it was happening. Not here, on the road in the middle of the most violent weather she had ever encountered, and where anyone might drive past and see them! She didn't know whether it was the very savagery of the storm that was triggering such riotous feelings, but certainly they matched it in intensity: her breathing as ragged and forceful as the wind, her responses as unbridled as the rain.

Only the feel of Dare's mouth assured her it was indeed happening, that it was all real. That, and the yellow beams of light she suddenly noticed sweeping out from behind the hillside some distance in front of them.

Immediately she stiffened. 'There's someone coming!' she gasped in horrified tones.

Reluctantly releasing her, Dare drew a deep breath, his lips taking on a wry curve as he too espied the approaching lights. 'Well, I can't say I appreciate their timing, but . . .' he reached out to touch her mouth softly, 'I guess I'd better get us home . . . before I lose what little control I do have left,' he declared expressively, and bent to switch on the ignition.

Teal could only nod, her face burning at the thought of her lack of opposition, her uninhibited participation . . . and in such unbelievable circumstances! Oh, hell, what had she started by allowing last night to happen? she despaired. Obviously, she couldn't let the present perturbing state of affairs continue: determined to keep Dare at a distance when he was absent, and doing just the opposite when he was present. Couldn't she see there was no future for her in having an affair with him? Hadn't she already travelled that road before? Her lips compressed resolutely. She had managed to cut him out of her life previously, so why not again? *Because last time you were able to take flight,* a traitorous voice in the back of her mind mocked, and had her worriedly chewing the inside of her cheek as a result.

When they eventually arrived at the farm, it was to find the car park deserted of vehicles, not surprisingly, if not of wind-blown leaves and twigs and small branches. The kiosk, as they passed, was also evidently unattended, the doors closed. The only sign of life was a flickering light coming from the Debenhams' house that they could just discern through the curtain of driving rain. Although it was the middle of the day, the light level was only that of dusk.

'By the look of that, it would appear we're down to candle power or some equivalent,' Dare remarked drily as they continued on to his own home.

Teal nodded, not at all surprised by the possibility that the wind could have brought down some power lines as well as trees, and only grateful her own car would have escaped any damage by being safely garaged beside the house. None the less . . .

'Won't that have an adverse effect on your operation here, though?' she hazarded.

Dare shook his head. 'No, the main pump delivering the water from the river to all the tanks and ponds is diesel-fuelled, and we have smaller standby petrol engines for anything else that might require continuous power.'

'I see.' She paused. 'Talking of the water . . . her lips began to curve wryly, 'it seems an appropriate time. Once it's passed through the tanks and ponds, then it goes back to the river, does it?'

'Uh-huh!' Dare's lips twitched. 'Along with a number of fry and fingerlings on occasion.' At her brow-lifting glance, he explained, 'When their tanks are being vacuumed to clear them of uneaten food, et cetera, a few of them sometimes get sucked into the pipe as well.' His mouth widened into a humorous grin. 'Just below the farm, the Calanda River can be quite a rewarding area to fish for trout.'

'In those circumstances, I suppose it could,' granted Teal with a spontaneous half-laugh. 'Although since your largest trade is in eggs . . .' She hesitated, her head tilting quizzically. 'That's what Laurie said on Tuesday, isn't it?'

Dare gave a confirming nod. 'With our suitable climate, pure water, and most particularly our freedom from the many viruses that afflict trout elsewhere in the world, there's an ever-increasing demand internationally for Tasmanian trout eggs,' he advised as they drew to a halt outside his double-storeyed sandstone home. 'But now . . .' He eyed the distance to the porch significantly. 'If you'd like to make a dash for it, I'll get rid of the car.'

With a rueful grimace for the second drenching she was about to receive, Teal drew a deep breath and reached for the door-handle. Her following race for the protection of the porch, despite the speed with which it was accomplished, still did not prevent her from being saturated once more. So much so, in fact, that after entering the house she remained in the darkened, parquet-floored entrance hall, reluctant to drip water over any of the other rooms' carpeting. Without a veranda or balcony to protect them from any flying debris, the windows had been shuttered, thereby making the interior even more dim than it would otherwise have been.

'What in heaven's name are you doing hovering here in the dark?' drawled Dare on finding her there some minutes later, his clothes obviously having fared no better than her own. And, after her explanation, 'Well, you could have gone into the breakfast-room, at least. That has a polished floor . . . and it'll be a damn sight lighter than here.'

Teal shrugged deprecatingly. 'It wasn't for long.' She paused. 'Besides, I don't know where the breakfast-room is, in any case.'

Dare's teeth flashed whitely in the darkness, and she suddenly found her hand clasped in his. 'Then allow me to show you.' He began tugging her along behind him as he headed down the hall and into a small but attractively furnished room at the rear of the house. 'You can wait here while I hunt up a lamp or two, then we'll be able to see about getting out of these wet clothes.'

An appealing prospect, Teal had to agree, and only then noticing what he was setting down on one of the chairs at the table. 'Oh, thank you for bringing my bag in,' she exclaimed in appreciative tones. It contained the culottes and top she had worn the day before. 'Now I have something to change into.'

'The thought almost makes me wish I'd left it where it was,' Dare promptly put forward with a teasing glint in his eyes, and she reddened helplessly at the provoking connotation in his words.

'In the meantime, however, neither of these pools of water is getting any smaller,' she just managed to parry at length, pointedly indicating the growing puddles they were both creating on the floor.

'While I'm not the only one looking forward to having a shower . . . right?' he deduced, accepting her evasion. 'But first I'd better find those lamps. We wouldn't want you unable to locate your clothes in the bathroom afterwards, would we?' He cast her another audacious glance, which had her breath catching in her throat, and took his departure.

Left on her own, Teal wandered over to the window, looking out absently through the louvred shutters at the rain- and wind-swept hills that rose behind the house. Sheets of lightning bathed them periodically in light, one particular clap of ensuing thunder making her flinch involuntarily as it reverberated overhead and a flurry of hailstones suddenly peppered the walls and shutters.

In actual fact, she wished she could just go home—if only to give herself a chance to really think things through without Dare being around to confuse the issue. For issue, read thoughts and senses, she amended derisively with a sigh. Nevertheless, since it was a working day, after all, she supposed she did have a responsibility to at least make an effort to get some work done if at all possible. Besides, she didn't particularly relish the idea of driving home in such atrocious conditions, in any event, she had to confess, ruefully.

'As incredible as it seems, I think it's getting worse,' commented Dare on his return with a couple of gas lamps that cast a cheering light on the room.

Turning away from the window, Teal nodded. 'I was thinking that myself,' she owned in whimsical tones. 'The ground is almost white with hail now.'

'Mmm, at least we were fortunate enough to make it here before that arrived.' His mouth tilted eloquently. 'It wouldn't have been too much fun if we'd had a smashed windscreen to contend with as well as all the rest.'

Teal grimaced and shivered at the thought, and seeing her action Dare frowned. 'You look as if you're cold.' Depositing one of the lamps on the table, he picked up her bag and, with an inviting half-smile, inclined his head towards the door. 'Come on . . . follow me, and I'll show you the way to the bathroom. You'll feel better once you've showered and dressed in something dry.'

Teal's confirming nod was explicitly executed and, with an answering grin, he began leading the way into the hall and up the curving staircase. 'You're probably hungry too,' he deduced as they reached the upper floor. Pausing, he sent her a bantering look over his shoulder. 'So if you're good, I might even make you one of my special trout lunches.'

Teal's mouth came close to watering at the thought. As a matter of fact, she did feel a trifle hollow inside, and she knew from experience just how delectably he could cook his favourite fish.

'And how good is good?' she quipped impulsively, slanting him a look that was partly provocative, partly dubious, from beneath her luxuriant lashes.

The vibrant gaze Dare bestowed on her in return had her swallowing convulsively and wishing she had simply proffered her thanks. 'In view of your wet and obviously chilled state, disappointingly I suspect this is not the time for answering such a leading question,' he drawled in meaningful tones, and continued a short way along the passage to open a wooden-panelled door and then step into the room.

Following, Teal entered the pale green and white-tiled bathroom somewhat more slowly, and found he had already set the lamp on the top of a strategically placed cupboard and her bag on the side of the vanity unit.

'You'll find towels and so forth in the cupboard,' he advised, starting back in her direction. Drawing abreast of her, he stopped, a hand beneath her chin tipping her face up to his. 'Just don't be long, hmm? Or I may be tempted to return and give you an answer to that question, after all.' His mouth closed on hers with a leisurely thoroughness that made her heart thump heavily against her ribs as the cool feeling that had encompassed her was rapidly replaced by a pervasive warmth.

A warmth that disconcertingly remained with her throughout her shower—despite her having locked the door after Dare had made his exit.

'Feel better?' asked Dare on an indolent note when Teal discovered him in the kitchen on her eventual return downstairs, and she nodded jerkily.

It was plain from his own change to dry denims and shirt that he had showered in the meantime as well. His tanned skin gleamed healthily, his dark hair only damp now, although still slightly unruly, the light from the lamp on the table seeming to intensify his rugged attractiveness. The picture he presented was vital, virile . . . exciting, and Teal's throat tightened as she felt his appeal tug at her emotions.

'Er—is there somewhere I can put these to dry a little?' she asked, mastering her voice with difficulty, and eyeing the wet jeans and T-shirt she held in one hand. In the other she had the lamp she had used in the bathroom, which she now positioned on a bench alongside the sink in order to obtain greater coverage of light.

'Through there.' Dare gestured to a door at the end of the room. 'I strung up a line in the laundry.' His mouth shaped crookedly. 'I'm afraid it's the best I can offer until the power's restored.'

'Which could be some considerable time yet, judging by the noise outside,' Teal speculated expressively as she headed for the door. The thunder and lightning were still making themselves felt as awesomely, the wind and rain continuing to lash everything within reach, even if the hail did appear to have finally expended itself.

'Mmm, Laurie said it's been like this ever since it started shortly after ten this morning,' he relayed when she re-entered the kitchen.

'Laurie?' Teal's brows arched in astonishment. 'You mean he's been up to see you?'

Extracting an armful of items from the fridge, Dare smiled and gave a negating shake of his head as he pushed the door closed again. 'Uh-uh! I contacted him on the two-way. Just to make certain everything was under control.'

'Oh, I see.' She nodded in understanding. 'And is everything all right?' Her glance turned enquiring.

'Fortunately. Although checks will still need to be made periodically, of course.' Sorting through the articles he'd taken from the fridge, he up-ended a couple of containers of ice-cubes into a bucket and buried a bottle of wine in among them.

'Champagne?' Teal bantered, noting the label.

Dare dipped his head in laughing affirmation. 'Naturally. Only the best of wines is good enough for the best of fish, and . . .' his tawny eyes held hers, 'the loveliest of companions.'

Teal moistened her lips with the tip of her tongue, wishing things could have been different, wishing . . . With a supreme effort she dragged her gaze away and, doing her best to make light of the remark, dropped him a mock-curtsy.

'Thank you, kind sir,' she acknowledged, albeit a trifle throatily. And in order to reduce it completely to to the mundane, 'Although to be honest, I would rather you feed me than flatter me. I don't know about you, but I'm starving!'

For a long, unnerving moment the room was stifling in its quiet as Dare surveyed her consideringly. Then, to her relief, upward curves made an appearance at the corners of his mouth. 'OK, precious, one trout lunch coming up shortly,' he allowed in drily drawling accents. 'We can't have you fainting from hunger.' He paused. 'Even if it is of a different variety from mine.'

The disturbing addition had Teal swallowing compulsively, her period of relief short-lived. 'Dare . . .'

'Relax,' she was told softly with a lop-sided smile. 'Don't you know cooking isn't an activity that allows for distractions?' He returned his attention to the items on the table, and she expelled a tremulous breath.

In spite of that brief disruption, however, the ensuing meal proved to be marvellous, Teal was to own later on, laying her knife and fork on her plate and easing back from the table with a contented sigh. Notwithstanding having been prepared on a portable gas hotplate, the fish had been succulent and cooked to perfection, the accompanying salad light but flavoursome, the bread fresh and crusty, the wine a delicious enhancement for the whole.

Even the conversation had been exceptional, she reflected. Almost as if, after having run the gauntlet of the storm, neither of them had wanted to shatter the protective calm inside the house with contentious words. They had elected to eat in the breakfast-room rather than the larger, formal dining-room, and she had wondered if the cosier atmosphere, aided by the lamplight, had perhaps had some influence on the matter too. Whatever the reason, though, she was glad of it, and it showed in her relaxed demeanour as she sent Dare a smiling glance.

'You always could cook trout better than anyone else I know,' she commended appreciatively. 'That was superb . . . and I thank you.' She raised her glass in a companionable toast.

Dare gave a deprecating shrug. 'I've probably had more practice than most,' he responded drily, an attractively deep half-laugh punctuating his words. He paused, his sable-fringed eyes filled with gentle raillery. 'Although, as I remember it, you didn't used to find the activity quite so praiseworthy.'

Teal's breath caught in her throat. It was the first

time they had touched on their past relationship, but since he had passed his observation so good-humouredly she resolved to reply in kind.

'No—well, at the time I guess my attention tended to concentrate more on the catching than the cooking of them,' she conceded ruefully. 'Nevertheless, I did still always enjoy them . . .' her expression turned contrite, 'even if I didn't say so.' She fingered her long-stemmed glass meditatively, and suddenly found herself owning, 'I suppose I did have difficulty in seeing past my own point of view at times, didn't I?'

The upward curve of Dare's mouth became more pronounced. 'Uh-huh!' he drawled laconically, and she gave a grimacing half-laugh.

'You didn't have to agree with me quite so readily!'

Dare flexed a muscular shoulder indolently. 'You raised the point.'

'Foolishly, obviously!' she retorted, but without any sting in her tone, and took a sip of her champagne. 'In any case, perhaps if you'd bothered to explain . . .'

'Would you have understood, if I had?'

Teal's blue eyes flew wide. 'Well, of course I would! I wasn't *that* unfeeling!' She hesitated, touching her teeth doubtfully to her lower lip. 'Was I?'

Dare leant back in his chair, lacing his hands on his dark head, his lips twitching. 'Let's just say, you held somewhat inflexible opinions on a number of matters,' he amended lazily.

More specifically, those concerning him! mused Teal with an abrupt spurt of dismayed self-censure. It hurt to have to admit it, but now that she was more secure in her own career—apart from Claudia snapping at her heels, that was!—she was able to see just what a perfectly infuriating little know-all she must have been at times. And not only that, but, as was so often the case at such an age, a know-all who actually knew very little. She shook her head in disbelief, her gaze turning curious as tentatively she asked the question that had been on her mind for some time.

'Did you also have the farm in mind when we were—still together?'

Dare nodded.

'Yet you never mentioned it.' Somehow the thought saddened her.

'Perhaps I should have, then maybe . . .' He broke off with a dismissive shrug, and when next he spoke his voice was humorously drawling again. 'Still, I guess you can take some of the credit for the farm's existence, even so. If nothing else, your departure provided the impetus for me to leave Tremaynes and strike out on my own.'

Teal frowned. 'How did it do that?'

Dare's mouth sloped obliquely. 'By removing the last reason for me to remain.'

Meaning her castigating insistence that he should make the most of his opportunities within the family concern, Teal deduced uncomfortably, and forced a shaky laugh. 'I guess you must have been quite relieved by my exit from the scene, then,' she quipped with protective flippancy, and drained the last of the champagne from her glass.

'If not by the manner of your leaving,' he surprised

her by unexpectedly mocking, and her mouth went dry.

'I—well . . .' she veiled her eyes with her lashes, evading his disturbing topaz gaze, 'I—I thought it best to make a clean break,' she excused herself in a stammering rush.

'Clean?' echoed Dare, sitting forward again, his bronzed and sinewed forearms crossed on the table before him. 'It was positively surgical!'

At the thought of just why she had made the break, Teal's breathing deepened, and when her eyes snapped up to his again they flashed with a bubbling resentment. 'Then it was doubtless no more than you deserved!' she retorted on an uncontrollably flaring note.

A muscle corded in Dare's jaw, his own demeanour hardening at her condemnatory tone. 'For any particular reason . . . or merely because the idea appealed at the time?' he fired back with heavy sarcasm.

Teal pressed her lips together, promptly regretting having permitted herself to be provoked into shattering the amiable atmosphere that had surrounded them. Not to mention already wishing she had ignored his remark. It wasn't a matter she wanted to be reminded of, and certainly not one she wanted to discuss.

'I'm sure you can work it out for yourself . . . despite your protests of ignorance,' she returned in a more moderate manner. Pushing to her feet, she started collecting their plates. 'Suffice to say, I may have been young, and even a little gullible, but I wasn't downright simple, Dare!' Notwithstanding her efforts, a trace of acrimony edged into her voice, and his eyes narrowed.

Grasping her wrist in a steely clamp, he stilled the restive movements of her hands as he probed tautly, 'You're claiming that I implied you were?'

'Well, not to my face, at least,' she had gibed before she could stop herself.

Dare muttered something violent under his breath, his grip tightening painfully. 'And what's *that* supposed to mean?' he demanded in roughening accents.

Teal drew herself up stiffly, defiantly standing her ground. 'As I said, I'm sure you'll have no trouble at all in finding the answer yourself . . . if you care to put your mind to it.'

'You think I won't?' His jaw set with grim determination.

She made herself return his gaze unflinchingly. 'That's up to you, of course,' she allowed with a pseudo-indifferent shrug. Sucking in a deep breath, she continued hurriedly, 'Meanwhile, however . . .' She tried to drag her arm free, but his fingers only gripped all the more inflexibly, reducing her attempts to a merely impotent glare. 'You're hurting!' Her voice turned stormy.

'While only you're allowed that privilege, eh?' Dare bit out harshly, rising to his own feet now with a perturbing swiftness that had her instinctively taking a backward step.

'I don't know wh-what you're talking about,' she faltered, startled by the unexpected and caustic charge.

'No, you wouldn't!' he grated disparagingly, his eyes glittering like shards of amber glass—the fact that they did causing tendrils of apprehension to curl along Teal's spine as she abruptly realised she had never seen him in such an ominously explosive mood before. 'Because the only thing you ever cared a damn about was your bloody work!' He shook his head, and her, as he dragged her closer around the table. 'Even our affair was merely incidental to you. Something secondary, to be considered only *after* your career!'

Teal moved her head from side to side in protest. 'That's not true!' she cried.

'No?' Dare looked so scornfully sceptical that she coloured guiltily, remembering how she hadn't meant for their relationship to interfere with her career.

'I—well, if that was the case, then why would I have become involved with you at all, and—and more specifically, why would I have—have gone to bed with you last night?' she defended.

Dare let out an irritated sigh. 'Heaven only knows—because I'm certainly beginning to wonder!' A derisive tilt shaped his mouth. 'Maybe as a pay-off for putting you in touch with Reece . . . regarding your work!'

Teal gasped. 'That's a lousy thing to insinuate!' she choked on a rising sob.

Releasing her at last, Dare ran a hand savagely around his neck. 'Well, what did you expect?' he demanded in taut accents. 'You've been coming on hot and cold all damn day, so that I don't know where I am with you any more! When I left you this morning I thought . . .' He came to a halt with a disbelieving shake of his head. Then, watching her anguished expression, he uttered a convulsive groan and dragged her back into his arms. 'Or haven't you yet realised the effect you've always had on me?' he muttered thickly, his lips covering hers with a scorching urgency.

For a moment Teal resisted as she felt his arms drawing her still closer to his hard and powerful frame, but there was no opposing the wave of hard-driven desires his demanding kiss so explicitly demonstrated. It seared through her resistance, stripped naked her deepest feelings, until all thoughts of denial—both of him and herself—ceased to exist, and she arched against him pliantly.

She couldn't keep fighting the consuming passions they aroused and, as a burning ache of longing began deep within, she gave a shuddering sigh of defeat and abandoned even the thought of trying.

CHAPTER EIGHT

WHEN SHE awoke some hours later, Teal stirred languidly, a contented smile touching her lips as she drew in the warm, earthy scent of the man whose long, muscular body lay still entangled with hers.

A gas lamp continued to give a low light from a chest of drawers across the room, although she couldn't recall it being put there. In fact, she wasn't even sure she could recollect just how she had reached the bedroom she now found herself in. Had she walked, or had Dare carried her? she wondered, her lips twitching.

The only thing that wasn't hazy in her mind was the memory of their fervent lovemaking. That she remembered very well—and the euphoric pleasure it had engendered.

Dimly she could recall them undressing each other; their satisfaction at the intoxicating feel of flesh against naked flesh, curve against hollow, hardness against satin softness. Dare had brushed his hands leisurely over her taut skin, across her flat stomach to her hip and the smooth inside of her thigh. To her soaring feelings, it had seemed as if her whole body was burning and throbbing with an ache that threatened to overwhelm her. Feverishly, she had arched upwards, her breasts pressing against his

148

chest, where the curling hair teased her sensitive nipples to prominence with its sensuous friction.

Her arms had slipped about his lean waist, her hands searching the rippling muscles of his shoulders and back, the length of his spine. His skin had been enticingly sleek and warm, and she had taken pleasure in touching him as stirringly as he had her, in tracing tantalising paths across that smooth bronzed skin with her mouth.

Outside, the storm had continued to rage, though no more tumultuously than the tempest she'd felt within when his lips had roamed her own receptive skin, caressing her slender throat and shoulders, then drifting lower to her full breasts.

'I love the taste of you, the feel of you in my mouth,' Dare had groaned rawly, raising desire-darkened eyes to hers as his palm had taken the place of his lips in covering her swollen and still moist nipple. 'It doesn't seem to matter how many times we make love, I always want more.'

'I don't think I'll ever have my fill of you either,' Teal had suddenly found herself owning in a shaky whisper, running her hands over his impressively developed upper arms. With a ragged shudder he had taken her mouth in a fiery, hungering demand that had sent what little was left of her wits spinning out of reach.

The surge of passion that had enveloped them both had been overpowering. Dare had made love to her with his mouth, his hands, his whole body, eliciting pleasures so intense that she had thought they would consume her; and she had responded in kind. For those moments he'd been hers, completely, and as they had become lost in their own world where nothing mattered but the delights they could give each other, Teal had allowed her elation to take over and she'd revelled in her total possession of him.

With rapidly eroding restraint, finally he had slid swiftly into her body, plunging to the deepest depths of her, filling her to overflowing with his warm maleness. Exalting in his thrusting weight, she had held him tightly within her, a husky moan escaping her as his hips rocked against her with each exquisitely prolonged stroke.

Then gradually the rhythm had quickened, their bodies straining together as they climbed closer and closer to the heights of ecstatic fulfilment. The climax had come in an explosion of trembling rapture, their hearts pounding in unison, their shuddering gasps of satisfaction absorbed against each other's lips as surging waves of mind-shattering pleasure pulsed through them.

Exhausted, Teal had descended slowly, relishing the protective feel of Dare's rugged body as he'd cradled her against it so gently. With his hand cupping her breast, she had sighed contentedly and wrapped her arms about him, and as sleep had claimed her a smile had softly curved her lips.

The same smile that was still there now as she turned her head on the pillow to study the man beside her.

In sleep, his clear-cut features were relaxed, his

overlong lashes gleaming against his sun-coppered cheeks, his tousled hair giving him a beguilingly boyish look—although there was nothing at all boyish in the steel-corded symmetry of his back, his powerful shoulders and arms, the strongly muscled long legs. The virile strength they exuded was totally and completely that of a man.

Against the sheets his bare skin was smooth, dark—and fascinating, she admitted ruefully. She couldn't resist stroking her fingers across his broad shoulders and down his tapering back, a pleasurable sensation warming her on feeling the muscles contract beneath the taut flesh.

'You keep doing that, and you know what the result's going to be, don't you?' Dare suddenly said sleepily in a humorous but somewhat muffled voice as he pressed his lips to the sensitive hollow between her throat and shoulder.

Teal's eyes closed momentarily at the pleasant sensation. 'You'll complain about me waking you?' she speculated in teasing innocence.

Dare's head lifted slowly, the gleam in his gold-flecked eyes as they met hers taking her breath away. 'No, that's not precisely the consequence I was imagining,' he relayed wryly, his gaze gradually darkening as he continued to scan her softly smiling features. 'Hell, I *like* waking up with you beside me.' His voice deepened. 'I always have.' Then, almost as if he could read her mind on seeing her expression change slightly, 'And you're way off beam if you believe I've even thought that about any other woman, let alone said it!'

Teal moistened her lips. 'Although there has been a considerable number of them,' she pushed out with difficulty.

Dare made a deprecating gesture. 'Not as many as I suspect you're disposed to believe, none the less,' he asserted drily. 'Sure, I've escorted a lot of women over the years, but you're wrong if you think that automatically means I also slept with them all.' His mouth tilted crookedly. 'You might at least give me credit for being a little more discriminating, not to mention in command of my instincts, than that.' He touched a finger to her mouth, drawing it slowly along the inner softness of her lower lip. 'It's only ever been you who's tested my powers of self-control to the limit.'

Just as he was doing to hers now, thought Teal, as she found herself wanting him to replace that sensuously caressing finger with his tongue, and she shook her head helplessly. 'Oh, Dare . . .'

'My thoughts exactly!' His voice dropped to a husky pitch, and with a groan he lowered his mouth to hers in a drugging, probing possession that consummately fulfilled her previous wish. 'And—oh, I wish I could stay with you longer,' he growled some long minutes later, beginning to drag himself away from her.

It was all so unexpected that Teal could only stare at him in confusion.

'Y-you're going?' she faltered.

In the process of moving to the side of the bed, Dare

turned back to her with a rueful curve edging across his lips. 'Again, not from choice, I can assure you,' he averred expressively. 'But the storm does appear to have abated at last . . .' there was only the sound of light rain coming from outside now, '. . . and as much as I would prefer to stay, unfortunately I really should inspect the place while there's still some light to see by.'

Teal nodded in understanding, abruptly realising just how late in the day it was. 'I—I guess I'd better be going too, then,' she murmured with a sudden feeling of self-consciousness, preparing to slide her feet to the floor.

'For crying out loud, why?' Dare promptly demanded, a hand on her arm propelling her back to the centre of the bed. His eyes softened as they searched hers watchfully, and he quizzed on a gentle note, 'Do you want to leave?'

Teal swallowed. 'I—well, my parents will be expecting me,' she evaded, reluctant to answer that question, even to herself.

'So ring them, and tell them you'll be staying the night,' he urged persuasively, and she drew a ragged breath.

'I can't do that!'

'Why not?'

She bent her head. 'Well, I mean, there's Amy to consider, for a start.'

'*Amy?*' Dare echoed incredulously, staring at her askance. 'What in hell has she got to do with it?'

Teal eased her tongue out to wet the surface of her

lips. 'I—er—well, she's already made it plain how she feels about you, and—and I wouldn't like to be the cause of . . .'

'And if you think I'm going to allow a seventeen, *going on thirty-year-old* to come between *us*, you're out of your mind!' he interjected drily, sliding a caressing hand to her nape.

Valiantly attempting to ignore the feelings he was arousing, Teal shook her head. 'But I can't just stay the night, Dare,' she persisted. 'Wh-what would Martha and Laurie think?'

'Most probably that our private lives are our concern—only,' he replied dismissively, tilting her face up to his. 'But if it's important to you, I'll get Martha to act as—chaperon for the night.' His mouth slanted across hers in a lingering kiss that started Teal's heart beating faster. When he released her, his lips immediately shaped with roguish humour. 'Although I can tell you now, she won't be successful, because there's no way you and I are going to spend the night in this house and not share a bed.'

'Dare!' Colour suffused Teal's face. 'You're shameless!'

'Where you're concerned . . . yes,' he acceded uncontritely with a grin. Followed by the shrugged addition, 'In any case, there's more than a possibility you couldn't make it home, anyway. There's bound to be more trees down, and the road could be blocked—even by water in some parts.'

A point she had to concede, but she still ventured to challenge, 'A phone call to the emergency services could supply the relevant information in that regard.'

'While a phone call to your parents would make it unnecessary.'

Teal shook her head helplessly, a rueful half-laugh escaping her. 'You've got an answer for everything, haven't you?'

'I hope so,' he endorsed in thickening tones, his mouth tracing the vulnerable line of her jaw to her ear. 'So, are you going to ring your parents . . . or shall I?'

Teal's breathing quickened, her eyes closing and her head falling back as his lips continued their seductive assault. 'I w-will,' she acquiesced unevenly on a trembling sigh. A relieved sigh, she suspected, and uttered a sound of satisfaction when at last his mouth claimed hers instead of merely tormenting her senses.

Had there ever been a time when she had been able to resist him? she speculated ruefully.

By the morning the power had been restored, and if it hadn't been for the debris scattered everywhere and the various puddles—some large, some small—that lay on the waterlogged ground, it would have been hard to imagine there ever had been such a violent storm.

The rain had ceased altogether during the night, and in the morning light the contrast to the day before was unbelievable. Today the sun shone brightly again, and there were only a few high clouds to break up the blue of the sky, while in the trees and nearby bush birds called to each other once more as they dried their feathers in the warm breeze.

However, as Teal soon discovered, although some things were back to normal, others weren't. And that included the state of the roads. The major ones might have been only slightly affected, or cleared, but it transpired that, as yet, a number of lesser ones were still closed for one reason or another, those two of most interest to her apparently being under water in parts—just as Dare had surmised the night before.

Even so, she could still have reached her parents' home if she had taken the route back over the plateau, but that would have meant almost returning to Hobart before being able to connect with the main highway heading north to Launceston, and as Dare pointed out it would also have added some hours to the journey, plus over two hundred extra miles. In consequence, it had taken very little persuasion to have her deciding to remain exactly where she was for the time being.

Not that she had really wanted to leave anyway, Teal acknowledged. In truth, she had felt depressed at the thought of parting from Dare so soon after the utterly intoxicating and unforgettable night they had just spent together. And, just as he had vowed, in spite of Martha's presence, she recalled with an irrepressible smile tugging at her lips as she turned from setting the dishwasher going.

'Well, what now, chief?' she enquired laughingly of Dare, dusting her hands together.

Contemplating her animated expression, he shook his head ruefully and warned, 'Don't tempt me. I've got work to do.'

'It was work I was meaning,' she responded severely, but mirth sparkled in her eyes.

Dare grimaced expressively. 'More's the pity! You have a glow about you this morning that . . .' He broke off, expelling a deep breath. 'Hell! It shouldn't be allowed, what you do to me,' he declared on a gruff note, and looping an arm about her shoulders began ushering her outside. 'Come on, we'd better get out of here . . . before you distract me altogether from what needs to be done.'

For Teal, it was one of the most joyful mornings she could remember as she accompanied him and Laurie around the complex, first checking on each of the ponds and tanks of fish and ensuring that all the equipment was running as it should, then afterwards assisting with the cleaning up.

Most of the time, Dare appeared completely engrossed in what he was doing and his conversations with the other man, almost as if she wasn't with them, and notwithstanding his earlier claim regarding her being a distraction. But then he would suddenly rest a caressing hand on her shoulder, slant her a captivating smile, or lazily lower his ebony lashes in an utterly enchanting wink, to let her know he was far from forgetting her presence, and her heart would swell with unrestrained happiness.

Oh, how she loved him, this man who had stormed back into her life, sweeping all her objections before him, stirring her blood and rumpling her wits until her mind, her whole being, was filled with nothing but him.

The only matter to temper Teal's mood was a slight apprehension as to Amy's reaction concerning her overnight stay in Dare's home. She really didn't feel like becoming involved in a confrontation at the moment, especially if it only succeeded in creating more antagonism in the younger girl. At the same time, however, neither did she have the slightest inclination to even explain her actions to the proprietorial teenager. As far as she was concerned, they were none of Amy's business!

Not unexpectedly, though, Amy chose to view it somewhat differently, and made her thoughts known at the first opportunity she managed to catch Teal alone, while they were all engaged in collecting the debris spread about the farm.

'I thought Mum said you'd only be staying here for the one night,' she began in accusing tones. Her mouth curled derogatorily. 'Or are you just hanging around in the hope of impressing Dare by deigning to lend a hand . . . even though it's not needed?'

Teal pressed her lips together, and did her best to keep her voice level. 'No, I'm merely waiting for the roads to clear sufficiently for me to get through, if you must know.'

Amy sniffed. 'You could have gone the other way.'

'I could,' Teal was prepared to concede. 'Although in view of the extra time and distance involved, it didn't seem worth it.'

'Particularly when you could stay here and try to latch on to Dare instead, I suppose,' Amy charged immediately, but to Teal's surprise, with more sarcasm rather than the outright hostility she had expected. 'I saw you acting all familiar with him earlier.'

Teal swallowed. Had it really been that apparent? Sucking in a steadying breath, she affected a creditably nonchalant shrug. 'We've known each other a long time . . . as I've told you before.'

The younger girl's dark brown eyes flashed angrily. 'Yes, but how *well* did you know him? That's what I'd be interested to hear!' Abruptly, she gave a partly mocking, partly satisfied half-laugh. 'Still, Mum's presence put the brakes on all that last night, didn't it?'

Remembering the delirious experiences Martha definitely hadn't prevented, Teal hardly knew how she succeeded in controlling the rush of betraying colour that threatened to pour into her cheeks. 'It was certainly appreciated, yes,' she just managed to get out faintly, guilt swamping her at the barefaced lie.

For her part, Amy merely surveyed her scornfully from head to foot. 'Yeah, I bet!' she derided, and with a dismissive grimace took her departure.

Momentarily, Teal was too taken aback by the other girl's sudden leaving to even feel thankful. Quite frankly, she had anticipated far more questioning and rancorous antipathy. On finally realising Amy didn't intend to pursue the matter further, however, she sagged with relief—not only as a result of the cessation of Amy's discomfiting remarks and probing, but also because the thought that she might perhaps have been

forced to tell even more lies had filled her with dread.
She was sure that, sooner or later, she would have
given herself away somehow.

Nevertheless, when she resumed collecting the
branches and twigs that lay strewn over the ground, a
hint of puzzlement remained in her mind as to just
why Amy's comments should have been so few, and
less hostile than expected. However, as the morning
progressed, and she noticed the redhead more and
more often in the company of Dare's younger trainee
manager, she wondered—hopefully—if he could have
been the reason. It would certainly remove some
hassle from her own life if Amy's attention was
directed elsewhere.

By lunchtime most of the cleaning up had been
concluded and the operation of the farm just about
back to normal. As a joke, Dare suggested Teal might
like to catch their lunch for them, and in the same
light spirit she accepted the challenge. She had never
tried her hand at angling before, but guessed that, if
she ever had any intention of learning, she couldn't
have a better teacher.

'No, you took your finger off the line too soon,'
Dare advised with a laugh when her first attempt at
casting proved an ignominious failure. 'Here, like
this.' He stood close behind her, his arms encircling
her as he covered her hands with his own in order to
demonstrate, once again, the correct action.

Intensely aware of the way his hard body was
leaning into hers, Teal gave a rueful shake of his head.
Her attention span seemed to be about zero. 'I hope

you're not hungry,' she quipped meaningfully.

'Only for you.' He set his lips sensuously to the side of her throat, and she trembled.

'Dare! Everyone can see us, and—and you're not doing much for my concentration,' she stammered on a breathless note.

'Or mine,' he disclosed wryly, his mouth tilting, and with obvious reluctance returned his attention to her casting.

And this time she was successful; the line landing squarely in the middle of the pond. Bare seconds later there came a sharp tug that had her half turning to exclaim in excited disbelief, 'I've caught one!'

Dare smiled lazily down at her. 'You may not have for long if you don't put a bit of tension on that line.' He went on to caution hurriedly, 'But don't try to lift it from the water. Just wind it in steadily and I'll net it for you.'

Teal nodded and followed his instructions, watching eagerly when he scooped the fish safely from the water. 'I think I could get to like this,' she asserted with a grin once her prize had been swiftly dispatched and placed in the creel they had brought with them. 'You don't have to wait long for a bite, do you?'

'No, well, in their natural environment it's necessary to employ a little more skill and psychology,' Dare drawled. 'Here, there's somewhat more competition for food, and of course, they're accustomed to accepting whatever food is dropped on the surface.'

Teal made a graphic *moue*. 'While I was thinking it

was all due to my brilliance,' she lamented humorously, and took another look in the basket. 'Still, it is a nice size, isn't it?'

He nodded and fixed her with a steady gaze. 'Want to try again for an even better one?' he challenged, and she agreed so enthusiastically that he laughed.

In fact, she tried quite a few times more, a couple of her catches equalling the size of her first, but none managing to surpass it. However, she was pleased to note that her casting appeared to be improving at least.

'If you're not careful, I'll fish the whole pond out,' she warned jokingly as Dare baited her line yet again.

'With more than a couple of thousand fish in there, somehow I doubt it,' he disclaimed in whimsical tones. 'Besides, the whole purpose of raising them is so they can be eaten. So if it pleases you to land a few . . .' He shrugged indulgently.

Teal felt her heart flip over. 'All the same, I think this had better be the last, or you'll be eating nothing else but trout for goodness knows how long,' she replied, chuckling, and this time cast her line to another area of the pond.

As previously, she had no time to wait before a fish took the bait, but on this occasion the jerk on the line was much harder than any of the others, so that, immediately she had reeled her catch close to the edge, she sank down on to her haunches beside Dare as he netted it in order to check its size.

'Oh, isn't that a beauty?' she gasped, her eyes sparkling, as soon as it had been landed.

Dare's eyes continued to hold hers for a long moment. 'Yes—but then . . . no more so than the person who caught it,' he declared in resonant accents, and, cupping her head with his hand, brought her mouth up to his.

Momentarily Teal responded to the light pressure, but, crouched as she was, she shortly felt herself overbalancing, and eventually ended up toppling backwards on to the grass with a helpless laugh—a carefree sound that suddenly died when she caught a movement out of the corner of her eye and, turning her head, found Dennis—and Claudia—approaching.

Swallowing convulsively, she promptly scrambled to her feet, and stood nervously brushing off her culottes as she awaited their arrival. Understandably, Dennis was unsmiling, his expression even a little aggrieved. In complete contrast, Claudia looked like a cat that had just been fed a bowl of cream.

'Oh, hell, how am I going to explain that scene?' Teal asked despairingly of Dare before the others reached them.

Adding her last catch to the others, he flexed a muscular shoulder in a manner she could only call decidedly unhelpful, and smiled. 'Tell him we're going to be married,' he proposed in a lazy drawl, and her lips parted in shock.

Was he serious? The audacious grin on his face convinced her he wasn't, and her expression turned vexed. 'I can't say that!' she dismissed.

Rising lithely to his feet, Dare gave another shrug. Another indifferent shrug, Teal surmised. 'Then I

can only suggest you defend yourself with attack.'
Pausing, he arched a somewhat taunting brow. 'Or
does he always have another female on his arm when
he visits you?'

A fact Teal hadn't missed, and which now had her
chin lifting slightly at the reminder, even as she
responded with an acrimonious glare. Yes, just why
was Claudia with Dennis? she wondered irritably.

'I was interested in discovering how the project was
advancing, so I thought I'd drive up to Launceston to
see you,' Dennis began as soon as the necessary
introductions had been performed, Claudia's eyes
having promptly widened with interest as they took
stock of Dare.

'And you can imagine our *surprise* when your
mother told us you were staying *here*,' that girl now
chimed in gleefully.

Teal pressed her lips together and kept her gaze on
Dennis. 'It was only for the one night, because of the
storm,' she explained as steadily as she could.

'Although it's fine *now*.' Claudia again.

Teal's breathing deepened. 'Yes, well, some of the
roads from here to the city are closed.'

'We managed to get through,' Dennis pointed out
significantly, and Teal chewed her lip discomfitedly.

'I—I guess the water must have subsided somewhat
since early this morning,' she offered lamely.

Claudia gave a feline smile. 'You probably didn't
realise because you were—*enjoying* yourself so much
here,' she purred with such false understanding that
Teal felt her temper start to rise ungovernably.

'As a matter of fact, no, I didn't! Because until only a short time ago I was working—*hard*—to help clear up,' she snapped. 'As I would have thought you could have guessed from the state of my clothes!' Her sardonic gaze encompassed both Dennis and the other girl.

Claudia, at least, remain undeterred. 'Oh, in view of your *rolling* in the grass when we arrived, I thought it must have been from—another cause *entirely*,' she tittered, and cast a conspiratorial glance in Dennis's direction.

'No, I'm afraid that was solely my fault,' Dare suddenly entered the conversation to claim smoothly. 'Unfortunately, my method of praising Teal for her newly acquired angling accomplishment evidently wasn't the most suitable, and she overbalanced.' He uttered a wry half-laugh. 'I can assure you I don't usually have women falling at my feet as the result of a mere kiss of congratulations!'

Claudia's openly admiring gaze made it plain she wasn't so sure of that statement, but for the moment Teal was only too grateful for Dare having stepped in to care. Particularly as the remark appeared to have mollified Dennis a little too.

'And now that's settled . . .' Dare continued, seeming to have decided to take charge altogether, much to Teal's relief, 'perhaps you'd like to see over the farm?' He eyed both Dennis and Claudia enquiringly. 'You'll stay to lunch as well, of course?' His mouth quirked humorously. 'Thanks to Teal, we have plenty of fresh trout.'

Dennis hesitated, but Claudia, with her eyes fixed firmly on Dare, accepted both invitations with alacrity, thereby taking the matter out of the other man's hands. Teal, meanwhile, bent to pick up the creel and fishing-rod, preparing to return them to the house, and causing Dennis to regard her with a frown.

'You're coming too, aren't you?' he asked, and she half smiled diffidently, glancing at her full hands.

'Well, no. I've seen the farm before, of course, and I thought it would be better if I took these,' lifting the creel, 'back to the kitchen.' Another smile quickly came and went. 'Otherwise our lunch may not be quite so fresh, after all.' When he appeared about to demur, she went on rapidly, 'In any case, I'd like to clean up a little myself. With luck, my jeans and shirt will be dry by now, and I'll be able to change into them in order to look slightly more presentable.'

'Hmm . . .' Dennis contemplated her speculatively, and Claudia, managing to tear her eyes away from Dare momentarily, immediately took the opportunity to make another of her insinuating comments.

'But how *fortunate* that you have changes of clothes here. It sounds as if it's a regular little—*home* away from home for you!'

Gritting her teeth, Teal cast the other girl a mocking glance. 'Not chang*es*, Claudia—just the one,' she qualified sardonically. 'As Dennis is aware, Dare and I went to a meeting in Hobart on Thursday night, and I took a change of outfit with me. *Fortunately*, as you say, because we got soaked on the way home yesterday when we had to shift a tree off the road during the storm.' She paused, her challenging blue eyes almost daring the attractive brunette to add something further, and then, when nothing more than a disdainful shrug eventuated, said in an overly polite voice, 'So, if you'll excuse me . . .?' Swivelling on her heel, she started for the house with her head held at a resentful angle.

Damn Claudia and her malicious innuendoes, she seethed. And that went for Dennis as well, for having brought her with him, anyway! The project was nothing at all to do with Claudia, and she had no business being there! For some time now she had been a complication Teal could have done without, but of late she was becoming even worse. Why couldn't she simply be satisfied with her own work and male friends, instead of attempting to take over Teal's all the time? In both categories!

CHAPTER NINE

BY THE TIME she had showered and donned her now washed and dried jeans and T-shirt, Teal had regained a considerable amount of her composure. When the others arrived at the house, and Dare excused himself for a short period in order to wash and change too, it enabled her to discuss with Dennis both the project and her attendance at the Tremaynes' meeting in something akin to her more usual businesslike fashion.

'Well, that certainly sounds as if it could hold some promise,' Dennis enthused on hearing of her talk with Dare's brother and father, and seeming pleased about something for the first time since arriving. 'It would have been better if they'd actually offered us something specific, of course . . . but I guess an agreement to consider us is better than nothing.'

'Mmm . . . maybe Teal's influence just doesn't stretch that far—*yet*,' put in Claudia meaningfully, but to Teal's relief Dennis was too engrossed in the subject of work to pay attention to her, for once, and went on to discuss the farm project instead.

However, even there Claudia was obviously determined to make her presence felt by continually sprinkling such remarks as, 'Do you really think that's the best method to employ?' or, 'That's not the way I would do it at all,' amid Teal's disclosure of her system and programming plans.

Fortunately, however, Dennis proved to be in favour of Teal's ideas on the subject, and as soon as Dare put in an appearance again, Claudia promptly followed him into the kitchen in something of a huff.

'Do you cook all your own meals?' Teal heard her ask him, and grimaced inwardly at the oozing tone.

'No, only breakfast, or those containing trout,' it was also possible to hear Dare divulge lightly with a laugh. 'Martha—you met her in the hatchery—kindly does the honours every other time.'

Now it was a softly coquettish laugh that floated through to the office where Teal and Dennis were seated. 'You obviously need a wife,' Claudia cooed.

Straining to hear Dare's reply, Teal suddenly realised Dennis was talking, and reluctantly had to force her attention away from the couple in the kitchen. 'I'm sorry. What were you saying?'

Dennis hesitated, then repeated stiffly, 'I said . . . you appear to be getting along with Tremayne better than you expected.'

Teal coloured, and avoided his eyes. Oh, lord, how could she ever explain? She felt so damned guilty! Drawing a shaky breath, she temporised, 'Yes—well, I try to keep my mind on work as much as possible.' And she had tried! she defended to herself. She really had!

'When we arrived, you appeared to have no objection to him kissing you either.'

Teal circled her lips with her tongue. 'I—he . . .' She hunched a slender shoulder. 'It was only a moment's light-hearted fun connected with the fishing.'

Dennis looked somewhat sceptical. 'You're certain of that?'

Certain? Right at the moment there were only two things of which she was certain: the strength of her feelings for Dare, and the perturbing fact that she now had two men in her life. One whom she respected and didn't want to hurt; the other capable of tearing her heart to shreds again.

'You don't believe me?' she countered at length, evading the issue once more. A trilling laugh came from the kitchen, aggravating her and making her question somewhat testily, 'Or is it that you simply prefer to believe Claudia these days? I mean, just why *is* she with you, Dennis?'

He made an indeterminate gesture, looking surprised. 'When she heard I intended driving up to see you, she asked if she could come along in order to see the damage the storm caused, that's all,' he told her matter-of-factly. 'We only got the rain in Hobart, not the wind.'

Teal's mouth shaped sardonically. 'Claudia's own car being out of action for such an excursion, I presume?'

His brows lifted. 'I—well, to be honest, I never gave it a thought,' he owned in a slightly chagrined vein.

'When she said she would also be company for the drive, I—just accepted it.' His manner became more positive. 'And she was good company.'

'Oh, I've no doubt she ensured she was,' Teal responded drily, suspecting he was implying, unlike *she* had been since his arrival. 'Claudia's nothing if not thorough.'

Dennis shrugged. 'I can't see anything wrong with that. Particularly in our line of work.'

'No, I guess not,' she conceded with a rueful sigh. It was so typical of Dennis to relate everything back to work.

Why, even his trip today had apparently been prompted by a desire to find out how the farm project was progressing, rather than any stated wish to actually see herself, she recalled wryly. And, with that kind of outlook, it was doubtful he was ever going to realise how manipulative Claudia was attempting to be on a personal level. If it didn't concern work, it barely interested him, and to be truthful she had often thought he had envisaged their own relationship more in the form of a business partnership than anything else. Certainly their conversations had usually seemed to centre on their profession.

Nevertheless, if Teal had thought Dennis and Claudia's unexpected arrival discomposing, it was nothing compared to the feelings she experienced during lunch. Having changed into a pair of dark brown trousers and matching silk-knit, short-sleeved shirt that seemed to emphasise his devil-may-care amber eyes, Dare looked dark and vital, but although

Teal could understand Claudia's evident interest in him she fiercely resented it, too. The more so when Dare appeared to do nothing to discourage her.

'It's truly amazing the rapport the two of us struck in the kitchen,' Claudia crowed soon after they were all seated at the table, in the dining-room on this occasion. 'I seemed to know instinctively what you required next, didn't I, Dare?' She laid an immaculately manicured hand familiarly over his.

'Mmm, you were a great help,' he acceded indolently, and failing to immediately extricate himself from her grasp, Teal noted with some asperity.

And so it continued, Claudia hardly taking her eyes from Dare throughout the meal as she oohed and aahed over his culinary ability, and generally did her best to monopolise his attention with gushing conversation.

Conversely, Teal became more and more tense as the meal progressed. She felt guilty about Dennis; she was—how could she deny it?—as jealous as hell regarding Claudia; and utterly devastated by Dare apparently returning the other girl's interest as he banteringly responded to her flirtatious overtures.

It was history repeating itself! Teal despaired, and it revived all her old feelings of betrayal and desolation. He would never change, and she had been a naïve fool to have hoped, for even a moment, that this time it just might have been different! Everything he had said or done had been a farce. They were merely calculated, practised responses, designed to play on her emotions in order to achieve his own ends. And she, like some lovesick schoolgirl, had fallen for them—*again*!

Naturally enough, Claudia was in no hurry to leave either once lunch was concluded. Eventually, however, when Dennis impatiently collected his vehicle from the car park and deliberately left it idling beside the front porch, she had no choice but to take her leave and assume her seat beside him.

'So how long do you think it will be before you're finished here?' Dennis asked Teal before setting the car in motion, and she hunched a shoulder indecisively.

'I'm not sure at the moment. It could depend on the delivery dates for the equipment. But it will be as short as possible, I can promise you that,' she vowed with a depth of feeling that obviously took him aback a little.

Recovering, he nodded in satisfaction and smiled. 'I'll leave you to it, then.' The car began moving, but only travelled a foot or so before stopping again, and he hazarded tentatively, 'You'll also be heading for home shortly?'

'Immediately!' she amended vehemently, and with another smile he accelerated down the driveway.

'And might I ask just what that was all about?' Dare promptly questioned guardedly behind her.

Standing her tallest, Teal turned slowly. 'Let's just say I've come to my senses at long, long last!' she gibed on a rancorous note, stepping past him and into the hallway.

She was brought up short by a steely hand gripping her shoulder, and propelling her into the sitting-room when she would have made for the office. 'No, don't let's say that. Let's try the truth . . . for a change!' Dare bit out corrosively, his mouth a thin line of exasperation. 'Like . . . you're panicking once more at the thought of actually sharing a part of yourself with someone, of becoming involved with a person instead of just your damned work, and as per normal when something threatens the cosy little world you hide in, you want to cut and run . . . again!'

'That's not true!' she denied fiercely, her hands clenching. Pulling backwards, she wrenched free of his hold. 'Nor am I your property either, to be detained as and when it pleases you!'

'So stop me.' The invitation was laced with harsh mockery.

Teal shook her head helplessly, as aware as he was that she hadn't a hope of doing as he suggested. 'You're a despicable bastard!' she choked, her eyes filling with the tears that had been threatening since lunch.

Watching her, Dare ground out a smothered curse, and raked a hand irritably through his hair. 'And you're a capricious little bitch!' he censured savagely. 'Just what did Elford say to you in the office, for pete's sake, to have you changing so suddenly?'

Teal struggled for some vestige of control. 'He didn't say anything! Unlike Claudia, of course!' Her sarcasm came through clearly. 'We all heard the flattering and teasing little comments she had to make! And you just lapped them up, didn't you?' she flayed scathingly.

Dare hissed out his breath, his body hard and tense. 'Did I?' A muscle jumped in his jaw. 'So what did you expect me to do? Ignore her? Tell her to confine her amatory approaches to Elford? I'm sure you would have appreciated that!' he derided in caustic tones. 'I also find it strange that her malicious little insinuations regarding yourself are a cause for indignation, yet when they're directed towards me you automatically believe them implicitly!' At Teal's disdainful look, he continued with a cutting edge to his voice, 'I might also remind you that you didn't precisely act as if there was nothing between you and Elford any more, either!'

Her chin lifted defiantly. 'I didn't want to hurt his feelings.'

'While mine are of no account—as usual!'

'Do you even have any?' she sniped.

Dare stiffened, the turbulent topaz of his eyes, the very set of his shoulders, portraying an aggression that was ominous. 'Implying?' he probed in a deadly tone, his hands resting on his lean hips.

A shiver of apprehension chased up Teal's spine, the atmosphere in the room so thick with tension that she felt unable to breathe. 'Well, any of—of loyalty,' she half blurted, half charged in a nervous rush.

'Loyalty?' Dare's anger exploded into disbelief. 'Allow me to refresh your memory with the fact that it's *you* who has the penchant for desertion!'

Teal's colour rose. 'With good reason!' she defended.

'That's yet to be established,' he disputed, tight-lipped. 'Even the idea that I might be interested in your clinging colleague is bloody ludicrous!' His eyes ranged over her coldly. 'You seem to have conveniently forgotten that ICS still has a commission to complete here . . . and my brutally telling a member of their staff that she would be better keeping her undesirable advances for someone who might welcome them is not exactly conducive to good business relations!' Taking an audible breath, he ran a hand wearily around his neck. 'In the name of heaven, why would I even give her a second look when I had you?'

Teal pressed her lips together, fighting desperately to retain her defences against the undermining appeal in his words. 'Well, if it wasn't Claudia, doubtless it would soon be someone else,' she retorted with acid bitterness.

Dare's amber eyes flared. 'Is that so?' He caught her chin and dragged it up. 'Well, let me tell you something, my pet,' he grated. 'Foolishly, I'm beginning to suspect, but I never even looked at another woman, let alone touched one, while we were together. They just didn't interest me.'

'*Liar!*' The word burst rawly from Teal's lips to hang in the electrically charged air like a whiplash, and Dare went rigid, as if he had just been stung by the very same whip.

'If that's what you've decided, then I'm obviously wasting my time,' he said at length on an unexpectedly flat note, his expression taut, unreadable, and turning on his heel he made for the doorway.

Confused by his reaction, Teal chewed at her lip as she watched him. There was nothing to stop her leaving now, and she should have been relieved, but as he reached the opening a panicky feeling invaded her stomach that wouldn't be denied, and she knew she couldn't leave it as it was.

'Well, you know it's the truth!' she cried brokenly.

Although he stopped, Dare didn't turn. 'So you've apparently decided,' he merely reiterated with a shrug, and resumed walking.

Tears burnt at the back of Teal's eyes. 'What about . . . Patrice Holloway, then?' Anguishedly, she finally said the name that had been the cause of so much misery over the years.

At that, Dare both halted and swung round. 'Patrice!' he echoed incredulously, taking a few steps forward.

Teal drew a shuddering breath. 'Th-then you do at least admit to kn-knowing her,' she whispered tremulously.

He flexed a shoulder in a dismissive gesture, continuing to retrace his steps. 'Sure, I know her.' Pausing, he frowned. 'What I don't know is . . . what on earth she's got to do with any of this!'

Teal shook her head despairingly. 'Stop it! Can't you stop lying even now?' she sobbed. 'Don't you understand, I found out about the two of you!' Feeling dampness start to streak her cheeks, she turned away, brushing at her face with her fingers. 'It—it was all there in b-black and white, in th-the newspaper . . .'

With a violent expletive, Dare spun her back to face him, grasping her head between his hands when she would have resisted. '*What was?*' he rasped.

Teal's lips trembled. 'Y-you know . . .'

'If I did, I wouldn't be asking!' he interposed impatiently. 'So why don't you just tell me precisely what you're talking about?'

She shivered and veiled her eyes with her lashes, steeling herself to sound dispassionate. 'The writer said they were pleased to at last be able to—exclusively reveal the identity of—of . . .' her voice began to break, but she somehow managed to master it, and went on '. . . the female who had been keeping the—dashing and very eligible Dare Tremayne out of circulation of late, and that it was none other than—than the luscious, raven-haired temptress, Patrice Holloway. The writer had seen the—amorous twosome dining by candlelight in out-of-the-way

restaurants on more than just one occasion n-now.'
She came to a quavering halt.

'And you *believed* that garbage?' Dare's harsh
demand sliced at her, making her eyes jerk up to
his.

'It—it was in one of your family's own newspapers,'
she stammered.

'That's as may be,' he was prepared to admit. 'But
the contents are still solely the editor's decision.' He
shook his head, the gentle look filtering into his eyes
making her heart somersault. 'Oh, love, how could
you have believed something in a sensationalising
gossip column?'

The tip of her tongue glided around the edges of
her mouth. 'You mean—you hadn't been seeing
her?'

'Oh, I'd taken her out for a meal on a couple of
occasions,' he granted offhandedly, and when she
attempted to turn her head away he forced her face
back to his. 'Although not for the reason you
evidently imagine,' he added urgently. 'I can also
assure you Patrice was feeling anything but—luscious,
or tempting—at the time, either. Her personal life was
in something of a shambles, and I was merely acting
as a shoulder to cry on—or a buffer, if you like—while
she tried to pick up the pieces. We've known each
other since we were kids, and she knew she could talk
her problems over with me without there being any
fear of all the sorry details being leaked, to the media
in particular, immediately afterwards.' His fingers
slid into her hair in a caressing movement, a rueful

curve beginning to pull at his mouth. 'Believe me, it was a delectable, blonde-haired enchantress who took me out of circulation . . . no one else!'

Teal quivered. 'Then why didn't you tell me about her?'

'Obviously, I should have done,' he averred wryly. 'But as far as I was concerned, it simply wasn't of sufficient importance to warrant mentioning. She rang me a couple of times, asking if we could talk, and I merely arranged for our meetings to take place on those nights when you were at college doing one of your courses . . . because not even for Patrice was I prepared to give up any of my time with you.' He bent to brush her parted lips with his own. 'And when we were together, my pet, you can take my word for it, Patrice was the farthest thing from my mind!' His voice deepened huskily, his thumbs stroking either side of her jaw. 'Hell, I wanted to marry you!'

Teal's breath caught in her throat, her widening eyes searching his in shock. 'You—really wanted to marry me?'

His mouth sloped crookedly. 'If only you'd stayed around long enough for me to ask you.'

'Oh, Dare . . .' Uncontrollable tears started to spike her lashes again at the appalling realisation that all the anguish of the past five years had been so completely unnecessary. 'If only I hadn't seen that article! If I'd maybe just said something,' she grieved strickenly, collapsing against him, and with a stunned look of his own Dare caught her to him convulsively.

'Good lord, that's it, isn't it?' he groaned, and, keeping her cradled in his arms, dropped them both down on to the velvet-covered sofa behind them. 'I didn't immediately connect the two . . . but that lousy gossip column is the reason you left!'

Teal glanced at him sidelong, her tearful gaze confused. 'Then why did—*you* think I'd left?'

Dare shrugged, his hands playing up and down her arms. 'I assumed it must have been because of my failure to treat my work at Tremaynes as seriously as you believed I should,' he disclosed on a ruefully released breath.

'Oh, no!' Teal shook her head in repudation, touching her fingers tenderly to his lean cheek. 'That would never have been important enough to make me leave you.' She hesitated, her eyes dropping slightly. 'Even if my remarks did apparently keep you there when you would rather have resigned.'

Dare frowned. 'What makes you think that?'

Surprise had her glancing upwards again. 'I—well, you evidently already had the farm in mind, and you said only yesterday that it was my—my leaving that provided the impetus for you to strike out on your own,' she recalled sadly.

Catching hold of her fingers, Dare held them to his lips. 'Yes, but not because you weren't there to offer any objections . . . simply because you weren't there any more—period,' he corrected softly with a smile that made her feel weak. 'The place held too many memories I just couldn't forget.'

Teal bent her head, her every nerve devastatingly aware of the warmth of his mouth against her fingers, of the hard and muscular length of his thighs beneath hers. 'I'm so sorry, but—but when I saw that gossip item I thought you must have been—tiring of me, and she sounded so stunning . . . as well as coming from your own social set. I—I couldn't see how I could possibly compete, and . . .'

'Oh, *love*!' Dare broke in heavily, his arms tightening about her reassuringly. 'You did more than merely compete . . . you surpassed! Dear heaven, I was in love with you . . . totally and irrevocably!' His voice thickened, his lips finding the throbbing cord at the side of her throat. 'I still am!' His mouth lifted to her parted lips now. 'When I discovered you'd gone, I nearly went out of my mind. You'd become a part of me, and without you I felt incomplete. Then, when I finally acknowledged that you really weren't coming back, I tried fighting my feelings, denying them, but in spite of all my efforts I still went on loving you. Nothing could stop it, and nothing ever will!' He drew back a space. 'And if Elford thinks he has a claim on you, then I can tell you here and now, he's going to have one hell of a fight on his hands!'

'Oh, Dare!' Teal wrapped her arms tightly around his neck, her fingers tangling in his dark hair. 'I've never felt about Dennis the way I do about you. I loved you so much, I was heartbroken when I thought you preferred someone else to me. I had to get away, try to forget you, somehow pretend it had never happened. Incredibly, for a time I thought I'd succeeded, until . . .' her lips shaped with soft eloquence, 'I set eyes on you again on Tuesday morning.'

'And . . .?' he prompted, his lips finding the sensitive area behind her ear.

She quivered, and a rosily self-conscious colour tinted her cheeks. 'Whereupon all my thoughts seemed determined to concentrate on . . . our lovemaking,' she confessed throatily.

'You mean . . . like this?' Now Dare's mouth met hers hungrily in a long, probing kiss that made her tremble, his hands moulding the supple contours of her pliant body as he began sliding her down against the cushions.

'Oh, yes! Exactly like this . . .' Teal just managed to endorse feverishly when his lips parted from hers in order to nuzzle a swelling breast—and while there was still time for coherent thought, before she surrendered completely to the engulfing passion he was so sensuously arousing . . .

As it happened, Teal met Patrice Holloway—or Patrice Aird as she was now—at her wedding, some six weeks later. But by then, secure as she was in the knowledge of Dare's love, all her previous anxieties regarding the other woman had been well and truly dispelled, and she had even—as Dare had suggested she probably would—found Patrice extremely likeable. Certainly there had been nothing in her manner to suggest she had ever seen Teal's new husband in the light of anything but a good friend.

Awakening one morning shortly after their return to the farm from their honeymoon on the Great Barrier Reef, Teal nestled closer to Dare's warm length and deposited a lingering kiss on his bronzed shoulder in return for the heart-stirringly tender look in his eyes as he regarded her.

'I made us waste five whole years—for nothing—didn't I?' she rued with a sigh.

'Not necessarily,' he reassured her gently, caressing her smooth cheek. 'At least it provided us both with the knowledge that what we felt for each other was lasting. That's more than a lot have when they marry.'

'Hmm—I suppose so,' Teal allowed idly, succumbing to her present contentment. 'Although if you hadn't, by pure chance, selected ICS to . . .'

'Pure chance, like hell!' Dare cut in whimsically, laughing. 'That was very definitely deliberate, I can assure you, my love.'

'So that time you met Dad while fishing, he did tell you where I worked,' she deduced with a gasp.

'Uh-huh!' he retorted with evident satisfaction. 'Until that day I had no idea you were even back in the State, and . . . if I didn't realise then just how I felt about you, I very soon did afterwards, because you have no idea how rapidly I came to the conclusion that the computer installation I'd been considering couldn't possibly be carried out by any other consultancy.

'With me handling the project?'

Dare nodded decisively.

'But what if I hadn't been given the project?' A sudden thought flashed into her mind, and she smiled widely. 'What if it had been given to Claudia instead? As I pleaded with Dennis to do when I first heard it was for you. If her visit here was anything to go by, she'd probably have made your life unbearable.'

'Although not for long, you can be sure of that,' returned Dare expressively. 'Because if you hadn't been put in charge, I would have very shortly found some way to rectify the matter.' Propping himself up on an elbow, he eyed her with suddenly teasing raillery. 'And I thought you told me you hadn't made any protest over being given the work here.'

Teal traced a finger across his smiling mouth. 'No—well, I didn't want to make it too plain just how shaky the prospect of seeing you again made me feel, did I?' Pausing, she made a graphic *moue*. 'Although I suspect you guessed, anyway.'

His smile broadened. 'Fortunately. It allowed me to kill two birds with one stone, as it were.'

'Such as?'

Dare bent to stroke her shoulder with his lips. 'Getting you to admit there was still something between us, and . . . not allowing you out of my sight now that I'd finally found you again.'

'The dinner and—and the meeting,' she deduced half chidingly, half humorously. 'You used them to apply pressure on me!'

He didn't deny it, merely qualified on a deepening note, 'Although more to keep you with me.'

Teal linked her fingers about his neck, drawing his mouth down to hers. 'I can only say I'm very thankful you did,' she murmured huskily, her lips parting to accommodate his.

'Even though it meant you resigning from ICS?' Dare questioned watchfully some long, disruptive moments later.

Teal nodded, her blue eyes still languid. 'With Claudia becoming more and more of a headache, I must confess it was a relief in some ways,' she owned. 'It was harder telling Dennis I was going to marry you.' She gave a wry little laugh. 'Even though I suspect his disappointment was more from a business point of view than a personal one. Still, I'm sure Claudia will be only too willing to console him—on both fronts.'

'While you're—happy with the idea of freelancing?'

'Oh, yes!' Her reply was unconditional. It had been Dare's suggestion that she put her skills to use in such a fashion, knowing how much she did enjoy her work, and the idea had appealed greatly. 'Or at least until we have children,' she amended. 'I'll have to reassess the matter then, of course. If there's going to be any conflict between the two, it's not going to be our children who suffer.' She raised a hand to caress his lean cheek. 'And I'm looking forward to having your children.'

Dare turned his lips sensuously against her palm. 'I love you!' he groaned in resonant accents, his head now beginning to lower to hers. 'When I said our relationship would be ending on my terms this time . . .'

'You had this in mind?' Teal hazarded delightedly, sliding her arms around him as he shifted over her.

Pausing momentarily, Dare gave a heart-stopping smile. 'You'd better believe it!' he recommended thickly, and for some considerable time no further words were necessary.

HARLEQUIN
Romance

Coming Next Month

#3043 MOUNTAIN LOVESONG Katherine Arthur
Lauren desperately needs help at her northern California holiday lodge, so when John Smith, handyman *extraordinaire*, appears out of nowhere, he seems the answer to her prayers. The only question—how long can she depend on him?

#3044 SWEET ILLUSION Angela Carson
Dr. Luke Challoner, arrogant and domineering, expects everyone to bow to his will. He is also one of the most attractive men Marion has ever met—which doesn't stop her from standing up for herself against him!

#3045 HEART OF THE SUN Bethany Campbell
Kimberly came home to Eureka Springs to nurse a broken heart. Alec Shaughnessy came to examine Ozark myth and folklore. Both become entangled in a web of mystery that threatens to confirm an old prophesy—that the women in Kimberly's family might never love happily.

#3046 THAT CERTAIN YEARNING Claudia Jameson
Diane's heart goes out to vulnerable young Kirsty, but warning bells sound when she meets Kirsty's dynamic and outspoken uncle, Nik Channing. Yet she has to support Kirsty, even if it means facing up to her feelings . . . and to Nik.

#3047 FULLY INVOLVED Rebecca Winters
Fight fire with fire—that was how Gina Lindsay planned to win back her ex-husband. Captain Grady Simpson's career as a firefighter had destroyed his marriage to Gina three years earlier. But now she's returned to Salt Lake City—a firefighter, too. . . .

#3048 A SONG IN THE WILDERNESS Lee Stafford
Amber is horrified when noted journalist Lucas Tremayne becomes writer-in-residence at the university where she is secretary to the dean. For Luke had played an overwhelming part in her teenage past—one that Amber prefers stay hidden. . . .

Available in April wherever paperback books are sold, or through Harlequin Reader Service:

In the U.S.
901 Fuhrmann Blvd.
P.O. Box 1397
Buffalo, N.Y. 14240-1397

In Canada
P.O. Box 603
Fort Erie, Ontario
L2A 5X3

This April, don't miss Harlequin's new Award of
Excellence title from

Harlequin Presents...

CAROLE MORTIMER

Award of Excellence

---

elusive as the unicorn

*When Eve Eden discovered that Adam
Gardener, successful art entrepreneur, was
searching for the legendary English artist, The
Unicorn, she nervously shied away. The Unicorn's
true identity hit too close to home....*

*Besides, Eve was rattled by Adam's
mesmerizing presence, especially in the light
of the ridiculous coincidence of their names—
and his determination to take advantage of it!
But Eve was already engaged to marry her
longtime friend, Paul.*

*Yet Eve found herself troubled by the different
choices Adam and Paul presented. If only the
answer to her dilemma didn't keep eluding her....*

HP1258-1

You'll flip . . . your pages won't!
Read paperbacks *hands-free* with

Book Mate · I

The perfect "mate" for all your romance paperbacks

Traveling • Vacationing • At Work • In Bed • Studying • Cooking • Eating

Perfect size for all standard paperbacks, this wonderful invention makes reading a pure pleasure! Ingenious design holds paperback books OPEN and FLAT so even wind can't ruffle pages—leaves your hands free to do other things. Reinforced, wipe-clean vinyl-covered holder flexes to let you turn pages without undoing the strap...supports paperbacks so well, they have the strength of hardcovers!

Pages turn WITHOUT opening the strap

SEE-THROUGH STRAP

Reinforced back stays flat

Built in bookmark

BOOK MARK

BACK COVER
HOLDING STRIP

10 x 7¼ opened
Snaps closed for easy carrying, too

Available now. Send your name, address, and zip code, along with a check or money order for just $5.95 + .75¢ for postage & handling (for a total of $6.70) payable to Reader Service to:

Reader Service
Bookmate Offer
901 Fuhrmann Blvd.
P.O. Box 1396
Buffalo, N.Y. 14269-1396

Offer not available in Canada
* New York and Iowa residents add appropriate sales tax.

BM-G

H A R L E Q U I N
American Romance®

Live the

Rocky ☆ Mountain Magic

Become a part of the magical events at The Stanley Hotel in the Colorado Rockies, and be sure to catch its final act in April 1990 with #337 RETURN TO SUMMER by Emma Merritt.

Three women friends touched by magic find love in a very special way, the way of enchantment. Hayley Austin was gifted with a magic apple that gave her three wishes in BEST WISHES (#329). Nicki Chandler was visited by psychic visions in SIGHT UNSEEN (#333). Now travel into the past with Kate Douglas as she meets her soul mate in RETURN TO SUMMER #337.

ROCKY MOUNTAIN MAGIC—All it takes is an open heart.

If you missed any of Harlequin American Romance Rocky Mountain Magic titles, and would like to order it, send your name, address, and zip or postal code, along with a check or money order for $2.50 plus 75¢ postage and handling, payble to Harlequin Reader Service to:

In the U.S.	In Canada
901 Fuhrmann Blvd.	P.O. Box 609
Box 1325	Fort Erie, Ontario
Buffalo, NY 14269	L2A 5X3

Please specify book title with your order.

RMM3-1

Harlequin Superromance®

LET THE GOOD TIMES ROLL...

Add some Cajun spice to liven up your New Year's celebrations and join Superromance for a romantic tour of the rich Acadian marshlands and the legendary Louisiana bayous.

CAJUN MELODIES, starting in January 1990, is a three-book tribute to the fun-loving people who've enriched America by introducing us to crawfish étouffé and gumbo, zydeco music and the Saturday night party, the *fais-dodo*. And learn about loving, Cajun-style, as you meet the tall, dark, handsome men who win their ladies' hearts with a beautiful, haunting melody....

Book One: *Julianne's Song*, January 1990
Book Two: *Catherine's Song*, February 1990
Book Three: *Jessica's Song*, March 1990

If you missed Superromance #386 • *Julianne's Song*, #391 • *Catherine's Song* or #397 • *Jessica's Song*, and would like to order it, send your name, address, and zip or postal code, along with a check or money order for $2.95, plus 75¢ postage and handling, payable to Harlequin Reader Service to:

In the U.S.
901 Fuhrmann Blvd.
P.O. Box 1325
Buffalo, N.Y. 14269

In Canada
P.O. Box 609
Fort Erie, Ontario
L2A 5X3

Please specify book title with your order.

SRCJ-1A